## "You still believe my brother was in on this?

"Every time I think I can trust you, you remind me why I shouldn't. We're not on the same side." Tabitha stood abruptly and started for the door.

Rory grabbed her hand. "We are absolutely on the same side," he whispered. "Tabitha, face the facts. Somehow, you and your brother are involved in this mess. Only your brother can tell us if he was a willing participant or not. I know that you are not. I want to find your brother and make sure he has the chance to tell us his side of things."

Her anger abated somewhat. "So what do we do now?" she asked.

"We need to go back to the safe house. Let me see what I can dig up. All you have to do is follow my lead."

"What else is new?"

## KIT WILKINSON

is a Phi Kappa Phi graduate, holding multiple degrees from the University of Virginia, the University of Tennessee and the University of Lausanne, Switzerland. After teaching for many years, she became a stay-home mom and started writing romantic fiction while her kids were napping. Besides writing, Kit loves hanging out with friends and family, cooking for lots of people and participating in almost any sport. She and her wonderful husband reside in Virginia with their two young children and one extremely large Labrador named Ernie.

# PROTECTOR'S HONOR

# KIT WILKINSON

Steeple
Hill®

Published by Steeple Hill Books™

STEEPLE HILL BOOKS

Steeple
Hill®

ISBN-13: 978-0-373-44356-7

PROTECTOR'S HONOR

www.SteepleHill.com

Printed in U.S.A.

In this world you will have trouble.
But take heart! I have overcome the world.
—*John* 16:33

To David, for loving me always, in sickness and in health. I love you this much.

And to my mother, for all her gifts, guidance and graciousness.

## Acknowledgments

Thanks to my fabulous editor for shaping this story into its current state. Thanks to Donna, Ron and Charlotte for their many hours of help. Thanks also to Darin Riedlinger for technical support, to Steve Bracciodieta of the Chesterfield County Police Department for his savvy on procedure, to Brendan Conroy for his Navy knowhow, and to the art department for the perfectly fitting cover design.

# ONE

Just three more miles.

Tabitha Beaumont struggled with each new step. After swimming one mile through a cold mountain lake then biking twenty-six through the Carolina Blue Ridge, her legs felt more like weighted anchors than lean stretches of muscle. Still, she trudged on.

For over three miles, she'd emulated the long, steady strides of the two seasoned competitors beside her—just as her brother, Max, had coached her. But when passing the little crowd on Hendersonville's Main Street, she hit "the wall." Her body could no longer maintain the unvarying clip of the other runners. When they started up the final mountain trail to the finish, she slowed and watched as the two runners pulled farther and farther ahead, leaving her to battle the mountain alone.

*Just three more miles.*

She needed to focus. But her mind refused. Every muscle in her body screamed to stop. Her lungs ached for air. Her heart pounded against her chest. Her legs felt limp and numb. The dark, steep path loomed ahead invincibly.

*Come on, Tabby. You can do this.*

Following a sharp rise in the path as it curved around patches of evergreens, she continued to grind her way upward. The August air lay dense under the canopy of foliage. Sweat dripped from every strand of her hair, down into her eyes, the back of her neck and the front of her chest. Slowly, she progressed.

"Beaumont."

The whisper jump-started her tired senses. She looked around, but there was no one in sight. She must have imagined her name being called. Her eyes sifted nervously through the thick forest. Her legs continued to churn over the mulched trail.

"Ms. Beaumont!"

A gruff male voice sent a chill through her body. She could not have imagined that. Crunching leaves and snapping twigs confirmed someone was near.

Again, she glanced back. Two men dressed in camouflage ran less than ten feet behind her. Where they'd come from or how they knew her name, she had no idea. But they didn't belong on this mountain. Only competitors were allowed on the trails. Today, all the entrances had been roped off and guarded by event officials. And who in their right mind would run a triathlon in full fatigues?

Fear zipped through Tabitha's tired body. Her overworked adrenal glands fired up and she doubled her speed, trying desperately to outrun them. But the men were not shaken. They stayed close, nearly flanking her and mumbling to one another.

"Number forty-seven," one of them said.

Tabitha glanced down at the black writing on her left arm. Her entry number. Forty-seven. *Why* did they know that? She didn't want to imagine. Instead, she ground her heels into the mountain path with what little energy remained and pressed on.

The men continued to close in. One of them reached for her elbow. As his fingers grazed her arm, her fear transformed to utter panic. Her mouth opened. She tried to scream. But only a tiny gasp escaped. Still, she jerked forward, slipping from the man's loose grasp as his giant paw fell away from her sweaty arm.

Nothing less than blind terror moved Tabitha now. She

bounded into a full sprint. Her head spun from the forced exertion. Her breathing fell short and shallow.

"Come on, lady. Stop. You know what we need." The evil in his voice churned Tabitha's stomach.

"Yeah," the other man echoed. "Hand it over."

Hand what over? Her mind clouded at their words. What were they talking about?

Forget it. She needed help. Frantically, she searched for other competitors, but she'd lost the two runners ahead and there seemed to be no one behind. How in a race with over one hundred participants had she found a gap? How could she have put herself in this position?

*Foolish Tabitha.*

All she could do now was pray and run. As fast as possible, she propelled herself onward. The thud of her pulse drummed in her ears. She had to get away. And still, they closed in.

"Come on, lady! What Max gave you…we need it."

*Max? Did they say Max?* They knew her brother?

Tabitha pushed on. Every step more painful than the last. In her fear and exhaustion the trail began to blur beneath her. A protruding root caught her heel. Her ankle twisted and she went down on hands and knees. Rolling to her back, she kicked out blindly, sending one of the men back a few feet. The other grabbed her by the wrists.

*Oh, Lord, please help me.*

Battling some kind of flu or major dehydration, Rory Farrell was having the worst race of his life. Bent over at the waist, he veered off the path to wait for the cramps and nausea to die away. A few racers passed. If he weren't so spent, he might have cared that this would be the first time in five years he wouldn't win the Hendersonville Triathlon.

Instead, he collapsed his large figure down the side of a birch tree and tried to relax his aching body. He focused on steady breathing, taking a moment to soak in the beauty of his native

Smoky Mountains. His gaze floated lazily down the steep bank of the mountainside, until it stopped at a most bizarre sight.

Two hunters carried a racer toward the foot of the mountain. A woman. Was she injured? It seemed unlikely considering the way she flailed around between them.

Rory stood then launched himself down the rocky incline to investigate. Something strange was happening and he had a gut feeling that he needed to interfere.

"Hey! What's going on?" he shouted.

The men paused to locate his position. The larger of the two turned, revealing a nice shiny handgun. A shot rang out and Rory's trained responses kicked in. He dashed for cover behind a tree. The bullet whizzed by, striking a nearby leaf as it passed.

Well, no doubt about it now. He was definitely going to interfere.

In fact, Rory no longer felt sick. Other, stronger emotions had driven that from his system. His veins pulsed with heated energy and his own innate sense of justice.

The men descended swiftly, dragging the female racer between them. She struggled violently. Another shot echoed across the mountain.

Rory continued to slide closer. Steadily, he gained on them, now close enough to hear her muffled cries and catch a glimpse of her frightened face. A face he recognized. It was the racer he'd noticed at the start—the one with the big brown eyes and great smile. The men had gagged her, further fueling his anger. He pressed on, forgetting the dangers he faced as he drew near.

Rory crept as close as he could, using large trees for cover. Then, he charged at the armed man, yelling at the top of his lungs. A rebel-yell attack. It worked, too. They dropped the girl and stood still for a full second before taking action. Rory moved in and grabbed the armed man's wrist. Rory pointed the 9 mm down. With his other hand, he struck hard below the ribs. The big guy went down and so did his weapon.

Rory kicked the gun out of reach and spun around as the

second man took a swing. Pain riveted through his body as the man's knuckles made contact with his face. Rory took repeated blows before landing a right hook. The little guy stumbled to the side. Rory retrieved the gun from under the brush. He aimed fast, but the men had already fled. Rory started to follow but hearing the woman moan stopped him in his tracks.

In a thick patch of fern, she lay trembling on her back. She had removed the gag but made no attempt to sit up.

He knelt beside her. "Ma'am, are you okay? Did they hurt you?"

Instead of answering, she closed her eyes while her body shuddered through another violent tremor. He reached a hand to her forearm to steady her, but she tucked away, every muscle tensed and rigid.

"It's okay." He softened his tone. "They're gone. They're not coming back. I got their gun. See?" She looked up, with large, unfocused eyes. Her face was so pale he feared she would pass out. "Really, ma'am. You're safe now. But…you're kind of scaring me. Can you talk? Can you hear me?"

With a sudden jerk, she spun around on all fours and was sick. The sight brought Rory a renewed wave of his own gastric unease. A discomfort he squashed with a quick exhale.

"Feel better?" he asked her.

She turned back and nodded slowly. "I—I didn't…" Her eyes lifted to his face and widened. "Your nose!"

Rory wiped his face with his forearm and glanced down at the blood. "Oh. That's nothing," he said. Although judging from the pain when he moved his head, it was probably broken. That little guy had given it to him good. "Don't worry about me. What about you? What happened?"

"Those men… They—they said I…" She shook her head and shifted her eyes away. Her lips pressed together tight and flat.

Rory let the questions go. They needed to move. Her story could come later. "You think you can get up?"

She stared back at him and shrugged.

Rory straightened, offering a hand to her. As her palm settled into his, a warm sensation rippled through him—not unlike the pleasant jolt he suffered when he'd spotted her on the lakeshore earlier that morning.

She pulled up and applied weight to both feet then collapsed. Rory shot his arms out and pulled her to his chest. No jolt this time, but he couldn't pretend he didn't notice her soft curves brushing against him.

"Okay. Take it easy. Where's the damage?"

"Right ankle. I turned it. That's how they got me."

Already she seemed calmer, her speech more steady. She hobbled back and pushed his hand away as if she didn't need his help.

He grinned at her determined efforts. "Ms.—"

"Tabitha Beaumont," she said softly. "And thank you. Thank you for helping me."

"Tabitha." He grinned. "I like that. A good strong name." He put his hand on her elbow, again offering his support. "Rory Farrell and it's my pleasure. Now, the closest place for us to get help is at the inn, just up the hill here. I'll piggyback you."

"Piggyback? No. I'm all right." She stared up the steep slope and again slid her elbow from his grasp.

"Look, ma'am, I'm a marine. Trust me. I won't drop you. I've done this sort of thing plenty of times."

She gave him a funny look then began scanning the area below. "You know, there's another path down there. We could go down instead of up."

Rory narrowed his eyes and flattened his lips. He wasn't used to people questioning his authority, especially in this kind of situation. "That trail leads to the falls. We need to go up."

Tabitha folded her arms across her chest—a stance which he supposed was meant to look defiant. The movement threw her off balance. Rory had to grab her arms again to keep her from toppling over.

"I promise it's better to go up." He pulled her close, forcing her weight into his arms, taking the pressure off her bad ankle. Her face scrunched up with disapproval, but he didn't release her. "Trust me. Let me help you."

For one moment, she quit struggling and steadied her eyes into his. "I'm sorry. I'm just nervous. I know I need your help."

A little too quickly, Rory lost himself in her large chocolate eyes. The urge to brush his knuckles across her cheek where some errant curls stuck to her smooth olive skin overwhelmed him and he shook his head to clear his mind. He should have been too focused for such a senseless thought.

"You're sure there's not another way?" she asked.

"Positive." He released her long enough to reclaim the 9 mm Beretta from the ground and engaged its safety. "We'll need to give this to the police."

"Police?" She blinked.

"Of course. As soon as we get back, we have to report this."

"Yes. Right. I'm not thinking clearly. Sorry."

"Understandable." He looked at the gun and then down at his flimsy bike shorts. "Could you—"

She turned a shoulder. "Here?"

He tucked the gun snugly into the back of her jogging top. Then he squatted for her to climb aboard. Her hand tentatively came down to his right shoulder blade. It retreated just as quickly.

"No time to be shy." Urging her bad leg forward, Rory knocked her weight onto his back and felt her slide into position. Two long legs wrapped around his torso. Her hands went to his shoulders. She left as much space as possible between their bodies.

The balance wasn't ideal but he lifted her easily enough and started up the mountain. Planting each foot securely, banking every step, he clung to tree trunks and slowly advanced.

"You okay?" he grunted, feeling the lactic acid burn in his thighs.

"Peachy," she answered.

"Well, I've got you. Just relax."

"Relax? You're kidding?"

"Your hands. Relax your hands."

To his relief, she extracted her nails from his flesh. "Oh, no. I'm sorry. I didn't realize. You must regret—"

He heard that familiar hitch in a voice trying to fight off a good cry.

"I don't regret a thing," he said between exerted breaths. "Now, put your arms across my chest and pull closer."

Tabitha didn't budge. But she didn't cry. Strong, stubborn, shy. He respected her responses, although the timidity surprised him.

"Don't think about it. Do it."

Once she did, Rory decided that despite his own exhaustion, he could have carried her all day. She felt light and for the first time in months, so did he.

The marine moved with amazing agility even with her hanging on to his back like a frightened kitten. When he'd come out of the woods screaming like a wild man, she'd thanked God that very instant for sending him. What would have happened if he hadn't come?

Getting up the last part of the slope proved tricky, but Rory managed until they reached the runner's trail. He put her down nice and easy then folded over at the waist struggling for his breath. The way he pinched at his side, she could only imagine the cramping he had suffered.

In less than a minute, a small group of racers passed. Rory stood and joined them.

"Got an injured runner here," he announced. "Could one of you send a golf cart for us?"

"Sure," one of them answered. A couple of them looked at her.

Tabitha glanced at Rory. "Go on," she said. "I'll be fine. You should finish the race."

He ignored her and whispered something else to the others. Again, they glanced back then moved on.

"Really. Go on. I'll be fine," she repeated, as he walked toward the tree that she leaned against.

"Are you kidding?" He smirked, wiping the beads of sweat from his forehead. "I'm done. I seriously doubt I could make it to the finish. Anyway, I'd be one lousy rescuer if I upped and left you here."

Tabitha frowned, but truly she was relieved. She didn't want to be alone. Even though he was a stranger and she hated needing so much help, the fact that he'd risked his own life for her made her feel safe and connected to him.

"Did you tell them about the attack?"

"Not in so many words. But I wanted them to get some policemen looking around. Those men could still be on the mountain."

Rory turned and stretched his back with a few twists. He dripped with sweat and his nose trickled a bit of blood. Regardless, Tabitha could see that he was an attractive man. The blue of his eyes reminded her of the ocean, deep and expressive. She saw something in them, in him, which gave her a warm, peaceful feeling she'd not sensed from many men.

"You should sit." He came to her. Putting an arm around her shoulder, he led her to a smooth boulder near the trail's edge.

She tried not to, but her back went rigid at his touch.

"Are you in pain?" he asked.

She shook her head then scooted back on the large rock. He moved in beside her, so close she could feel strength and heat coursing through him. She wanted to relax enough to lean on him and borrow some of that power. Instead, she trembled and blinked back the stinging tears that formed in her eyes.

A strong arm wrapped around her and pulled her into a cozy hug. Tabitha wished she weren't so stiff and unnatural because it felt wonderful—like a life force surrounding and filling her with energy and hope.

"Tabitha Beaumont." His slow Southern drawl, full of confidence and warmth, spread her name over an extra syllable or two. "You just rest easy. You've had quite a morning."

She nodded, barely able to keep back the tears. "What should I do when we get back? You said something about the police." Tabitha wanted to do this right. This time, she would report the crime.

"You see that cart coming?" he indicated softly.

She looked far up the mountain trail and nodded again.

"Well, we're going to ride to the inn in it. Then we'll call a detective and when he arrives, you'll tell him what happened. While we wait, there'll be lots for you to eat and drink. And I'm sure you'd like to call your family. Husband, maybe? How does that sound?"

"Too easy." She tried hard to conceal the fear from her voice. But the sympathetic look he gave her showed she hadn't.

"I'm going to help you. I'll be right there."

"Thank you." She forced a smile. "I appreciate it."

He smiled and started to help her up.

"You know," Tabitha added, "we can probably scratch eating and calling a husband from that list."

"Not hungry?"

"Not married, either."

Tabitha suspected a smile hid in those mysterious blue eyes.

# TWO

On the lawn of the Birchwood Inn, Tabitha sat under a grand white tent and picked at a barbecue sandwich. She knew she should eat, but each time she considered taking a bite, her stomach gurgled in protest.

Athletes continued to trickle through the finish line. The summer sun gleamed high above. Tabitha gazed over the opposing mountain ridge but had trouble admiring the natural verdure and its famous blue-green haze. Her nerves were shot and her head throbbing. She felt capable of little besides sipping water.

She did watch her rescuer with a curious eye, but that could not be helped. The poor man could hardly move through the tent. As soon as he'd walked away from her, event officials, commercial sponsors, a television crew and even some of the hotel personnel had stopped him. It seemed everyone wanted a piece of Rory Farrell.

Tabitha learned from bits of conversations around her the reason for his popularity. To her personal relief, it had nothing to do with what had happened on the mountain. Apparently, Rory was a native son of Hendersonville, and part of one of its most prominent families.

For a few minutes, she lost sight of him and turned her attention to the other competitors who'd joined her table for lunch. When she next spotted Rory, his eyes were on her.

Drawing near, he held homemade oatmeal cookies in one hand and an ice pack and aspirin in the other. He'd cleaned his face and changed his clothes. Tabitha welcomed him with a smile despite her edgy nerves.

"That's not fair," she said, pointing at his clean clothes as he emptied the contents of his hands onto the table. "I'd really like to change."

A few more fans passed, shaking Rory's hand and patting his back. When they left, he took the seat next to her.

"Sorry about all that. You'd never know I was just home three months ago." He passed her the cookie then the aspirin and ice pack. "This is for your ankle. I noticed it's swelling. The paramedics said to ice it thirty minutes, then off thirty minutes and repeat. And drink lots of water. That fixed me right up."

"I'm trying. And thanks." Tabitha leaned forward reaching for the aspirin. And despite his chipper speech, she could see that his attitude had changed since their return to the inn. He looked tired and worn down. And he most definitely did not enjoy all the attention he was getting.

"You look better," he remarked, his smile strained.

"Yes. I'm starting to calm down." She swallowed the aspirin with a quick gulp of ice water then pushed the glass back to its position on the table. "Rory, I know it's none of my business but…" She hesitated, not sure if she should mention anything so personal. After all he'd done for her, she felt she had to say something. "Well, I heard about your father. I'm so sorry."

His eyes connected fast with hers. A little moisture appeared in them as he nodded. "Yep. It was a tough battle with cancer. That's what all the fuss is about. Everyone loved my pop." He turned away and looked out over the mountains.

"You must miss him."

"Terribly. This has been a hard week, coming home again."

"So, you don't live here anymore? You live in Arlington?"

"Alexandria." He looked back with a big grin, pleased at the subtle change in subjects. "Obviously, you heard all sorts of things sitting here."

"I did." She returned the smile.

He leaned close and whispered, "Well, just a warning. Things have a way of getting exaggerated around here."

"Exaggerated? You mean your grandmother doesn't run Hendersonville? And you're not the town's greatest athlete?"

Rory laughed heartily. The wide smile and the deep rich sounds of his voice warmed her. "You know, Gram may actually run the town. At least, she thinks she does. But the other? That's a new one."

"Hmm. I also heard that you're some kind of special cop which confused me since you told me you were a marine."

"Former marine. Now, I'm a federal agent. I work for NCIS."

"N-C-I—what?" Apparently, she was supposed to recognize the acronym.

"Naval Criminal Investigative Service. Like the TV show?"

She shrugged and turned her palms up.

"We're an organization like the FBI but run by the navy. My unit conducts terrorist-related investigations. We also investigate serious crimes committed by or against navy personnel."

"So I guess what happened today was nothing for you?"

"I don't know about that. I don't usually run unarmed in front of a man with a gun pointed at me."

"Well, I'm glad you did," she commented.

"Me, too."

Tabitha locked eyes with him and felt her heart rate increase to some anaerobic rhythm. Oh, dear. Was she blushing? She fumbled for something to say. Anything. "So, if you're not a marine anymore, why the haircut?"

"Oh." He chuckled then leaned forward running a hand across the fresh buzz. "I don't usually—my grandmother likes it like this."

"Nice." Tabitha didn't stop her grin. It wasn't every day she met a bona fide tough guy willing to shave his head for his grandmother. "So, did the cops find those men on the mountain?"

"No. They're probably long gone. But the detectives will be here any minute and we can give them good descriptions."

She pressed away from the table. "In that case, I'm going to change."

"I don't think so." He grabbed her wrist. His eyes shifted toward the colonial-style inn with its multistepped entrance then looked at her bad ankle. "I'll go. Tell me what to get."

Tabitha took in a sharp breath, acutely aware of his touch. And it annoyed her that he was right about the ankle. She was in no shape to hop all the way to her room. She exhaled, showing her agitation.

"I'm just trying to help," Rory explained.

"I know." She dropped her head, pushed the loose wisps of hair from her face and smiled. "I left the key at the front desk. Will they give it to you?"

"Yep. I know the manager." He winked.

"You know everyone," she teased.

"The benefit of growing up in a small town. So, tell me what you need."

Tabitha sighed and gave into his offer. "Well, on the bed you'll find my warm-up pants and a pink Nike T-shirt. And if you could, grab my cell phone, too. It's on the dresser."

"Pants, shirt, phone. Got it." Rory's kind smile flooded her with an unexpected rush. He moved beside her, his eyes fixed on her bad ankle which he lifted and placed on the chair where he'd been sitting. He put the ice pack over the sore joint and gave her hand a little squeeze. "Be right back."

As he disappeared into the inn, she stared after him wondering what had just happened. Her fingers tingled where he'd touched them and her heart fluttered in an unsteady pattern. She hadn't had that reaction to a man in years. Had to be her overwrought nerves. Prayer could fix that.

*Lord, my head is clouded. Please be with me. The Lord is my rock, in whom I take refuge...*

The psalm brought Tabitha some comfort until she noticed two men in suits talking to one of the police officers assigned to the event. The detectives. She drew in a sharp breath as her thoughts went back to the attack.

She shut her eyes and tried to remember the details of the morning. What had the men looked like? What had they said to her? They had wanted something. Something Max had given her? But what could her brother have given her that these men would be willing to kill for?

Rory funneled his way through the hordes of people between the lunch tent and the inn. His mind swirled in a confusion of excitement and concern. Nothing like this had ever happened at a triathlon. Even as a federal agent, he'd only dealt with one case of abduction—enough to know they didn't always end well.

*God, thank You for using me to help Tabitha.*

A prayer?

Yep. He'd said a prayer and it had flowed out of him quite naturally.

Was anyone listening?

That he didn't know anymore. No one had listened when he'd begged for his father's recovery.

Lifting a hand to his temple, he mounted the narrow set of whitewashed stairs. His headache had returned with the bitter emotions. The happiness he'd experienced helping Tabitha over the past hour slipped away with each step.

He entered the small lobby of the old B and B–style hotel, passing several antique hutches and tables, all loaded with country knickknacks and crockery. Crossing the wide-plank floor, he headed straight to the check-in. The manager, a petite blonde dressed in a simple white linen outfit, gave him a wide smile from behind the front counter.

He returned his cousin's smile despite his heavy heart. "How are you, Terri?"

"Busy. But glad you came in," she confessed. "You've been mighty scarce this week."

"Yeah, well, you know…" Rory's jaw clenched at the truth in her words. Hanging out with family only emphasized the absence of his father. It had been easier to be alone. "So, I guess you heard a racer was injured?"

"I heard you rescued someone."

"Tabitha Beaumont, one of your guests."

A look of concern fell over Terri's face. "Ms. Beaumont? She's hurt?"

"Sprained ankle. Nothing serious. But that's only part of the story." Rory shifted his weight back.

Terri folded her arms across her chest. "Well? What happened?"

"Two men, one armed, attempted to abduct her."

"What?" The petite woman's gray eyes grew large and a worried look settled across her face. "I didn't know. I just heard someone needed a ride back from the trail. Where did this happen?"

"About halfway down. I know the whole mountain belongs to the resort so I wanted to tell you that I've called some detectives in. They'll want to talk to you."

"Certainly. This is terrible. I can't believe it. Ms. Beaumont seems so sweet. I had tea with her when she arrived yesterday. I enjoyed chatting with her. Do you think she's in some kind of trouble? You know, she's a lawyer in Charlotte."

"A lawyer? Really?" He'd not even asked. Come to think of it, he hadn't asked her anything. He'd been talking about himself. How had that happened? "What else did she tell you? Did she seem upset about anything?"

"No. Not that I could tell. A little nervous about the race. She said her older brother's into triathlons and talked her into trying one."

"This was her first race?" His eyebrows lifted.

Terri nodded. "That's what she said. Why?"

He chuckled. "She did well. She'd been moving along for a first timer…" Rory stopped his pointless comment. Where was his focus? "I—I doubt it's important. Anything else you remember? Was anyone meeting her or assisting her at the bike drop-off or the finish?"

"Now that you mention it, I recall her booking two rooms." Terri took a moment to pull up some records on her computer. "The other room was registered under the name Bristow. She canceled it a few days ago."

Bristow. Probably not her brother. Different last name. Boyfriend? Could this person be connected to what had happened? Rory pressed his fingers to the bridge of his aching nose, wishing he'd taken some aspirin for himself. "Did she say why?"

Terri shook her head. "No. Is it important? Is this what the police will ask me?"

"Maybe, but they'll also want to know about the grounds and security. How you handle the event. Stuff like that."

"Okay." Terri rubbed her hands together nervously.

"I'll go see if they've arrived, but first, Ms. Beaumont needs a favor. A few things from her room. Could you let me in since she can't get up here with her bad ankle?"

She rolled her eyes. "Always ready to help a damsel in distress, huh? Especially if she's beautiful?"

"Do you really think I'm that shallow?" Rory held his hands in the air, feigning innocence.

"No. But you have other issues." Terri reached under the desk and pulled out an electronic key card. Then she called another clerk to cover the front. "Come on. I'll walk you up," she said to Rory.

Together, they headed up the wooden staircase to the second floor.

"What issues?" he asked. "I don't have any issues."

Terri pursed her lips together. "Uh…you haven't been in a serious relationship in years."

"I don't have time to date. That doesn't mean I have issues."

"Whatever you say." Terri was shaking her head. Rory bit back a reply. Why did he care what she thought anyway?

They passed several numbered doors continuing down a somber, narrow hallway with a few sharp turns. Terri stopped abruptly a few feet from an open door. Golden streams of sunlight spilled across the corridor. Speckles of dust hung lifeless in the downward rays. The quiet air seemed eerie, far removed from the cheerful whir of activity outside the inn.

Terri frowned. "I can't imagine the staff leaving her door wide-open like that."

Rory moved Terri against the wall. "Stay here."

He reached under his arm where a holster would have normally held his automatic Glock. It wasn't there, of course. He shook his head and entered.

The room was small—just enough space for the mission-style bed, a small upholstered chair and a three-drawer dresser. The bed's white quilt had been thrown to the floor and the rest of the linens peeled from the mattress. A few articles of clothing lay willy-nilly across the floor and dresser. He found no cell phone, no purse, no suitcase. He moved over the hardwood floors and opened the door to the bath. There were no toiletries, not even a toothbrush or bottle of shampoo.

"Clear. Come in, Terri. Are you sure this is Ms. Beaumont's room?" He examined a rumpled T-shirt that had been tossed recklessly into the corner.

"Oh, my!" Terri's mouth dropped open as she entered the chaotic room. "Yes. It's definitely her room. I brought her up myself."

Rory looked under the bed. Clean and empty. He opened the dresser drawers. Empty. "There's nothing in here but some dirty clothes."

"She's been robbed? Let me call my staff and see if anyone knows what's happened."

"No. Wait here. In fact, call someone to stay with you. I'm going to find the detectives and send them up."

She nodded.

A new wave of anxiety washed over Rory. He didn't need to be a cop to guess that the burgled room and the attack were connected. Maybe the men after Tabitha didn't want her, but something she had? Maybe they wanted both?

At that, Rory flew down the stairs. He hoped leaving Tabitha alone hadn't been a huge mistake.

# THREE

"One man was tall, thin...blondish. The other heavyset. No taller than me," Tabitha said to the policemen.

Detective Jon Greenwood sat across from her, rubbing his gray beard. His partner, Hines, stood nearby taking copious notes. They had joined her just minutes after Rory's departure, exhausting her with their detailed questions. If the day had ended right then, it wouldn't have been soon enough.

"And how tall is that?" Hines asked.

"I'm five-seven," she said.

The taller detective looked up from his little white pad as if to check her measurements. "Five-seven. Good. Keep going." He returned to his note-taking.

Tabitha sighed. "The shorter man was bald. Or maybe his head was shaved, and I think he had a scar on his face." She paused and looked at the deep red marks on her wrists where he'd held her. Her mind flooded with old images—images of another man, one she'd known most of her life. He, too, had held her arms and made them raw. The memory unsettled her. "I'm sorry—I can't remember any more."

Tabitha banked her hands in her lap to control the trembling. She closed her eyes tight as if to squeeze out the unwelcome thoughts, but her focus was gone. The only idea she could hold on to was getting home.

Detective Hines stuck his pen behind his ear and took the

seat next to her. "Try to relax, Ms. Beaumont. The details will come back to you." He laid the pad aside and removed his jacket. "You're shivering. Here. Take this."

"Thank you." She placed the tan sport coat across her chest and tucked her arms underneath.

"You mentioned the men wanted something from you," Hines said. "Any idea what?"

"I don't—" She shook her head. "I don't think they said exactly."

"But they named your brother?" Greenwood asked.

"I thought so. But my mind was on Max anyway since he's been coaching me for the race."

"And your brother's a dentist?"

She nodded. "Yes. In Richmond."

"We'll need his number and address."

"Sure. He'll get a kick out it if you call him." She rattled off the numbers while Hines recorded them in his notebook.

"Hope I didn't miss much." Rory appeared at the table. Greenwood and Hines gave him hearty handshakes.

"We miss your pop," Greenwood relayed. "The new chief is good, but he's no James Farrell." Hines nodded in agreement.

Tabitha's heart sank as she watched Rory's jaw tighten. His dad had been chief of police. No wonder everyone fussed over his absence.

Stepping around the detectives, he pushed toward her.

She returned Hines's coat and checked Rory's arms for her clothing. But his hands were empty. "You couldn't get into my room, could you?"

"No. I got in." Rory turned his head so that the detectives could hear. "I went up with Terri Patton, the manager. When we got there, the door was already open and most of your things were—I'm sorry, Tabitha—they were missing."

Tabitha's sick stomach and throbbing head intensified. She could barely swallow. "Room two-zero-seven? Are you sure?"

Rory nodded. "The room was ransacked. Basically cleaned out." He turned back to the detectives. "Terri's waiting for you to take a look."

"Sure. I think Ms. Beaumont could use a break now, anyway. You two stay here," Greenwood instructed, as he turned for the inn. Hines followed.

"My car," Tabitha whispered as she leaped from her seat.

The ice pack tumbled to the ground and she hopped on her good leg toward the edge of the tent. The idea of being trapped on that mountain, not able to get home, suffocated her.

"Ms. Beaumont, don't trouble yourself. We'll check it out," Greenwood called after her.

Tabitha didn't stop. She slipped past Rory's grasp and continued until she reached the grassy area in front of the parking. If someone had taken almost everything from her room, then they could have the keys to her car. She searched through the hubbub of activity, scanning the small gravel lot.

"Is it there?" Rory's voice sounded behind her low and stern.

She shook her head then turned to face the three men who had moved in behind her. Biting her lower lip to hold her tears at bay, she hobbled to the nearest table for support.

"A blue Toyota 4Runner. North Carolina plates." She took in a ragged breath. Then to Hines, she gave a full description of her SUV. Afterward, she glanced across the lot again, but the car was gone. She had nothing—no money, no phone, no car. She could feel what little bit of inner strength she still possessed fading away.

*Oh, Lord, why is this happening? Please give me Your strength.*

As the detectives headed up the stairs to the inn, Tabitha hopped back to her table still trying desperately not to cry. Rory moved beside her but didn't offer his help. She propped her foot up and replaced the ice pack, wishing he'd leave her alone. She felt too aware of him.

"Shouldn't you go with them?" she asked. "Since you're an agent and all that." *Please go, so I can think and not cry in front of you.*

"I'm not going anywhere," he said. His frown deepened as he took the seat beside her. His eyes, the ones that had warmed her a few minutes earlier, had turned cold.

He leaned back in the chair. With a slow deliberate move, he folded his arms across his broad chest. "So, Ms. Beaumont, it seems some pretty serious people are after you. I think you should tell me why. I mean, up until now you've been fairly calm, but you find out your car's gone and you kind of lose it. Why is that? Why don't you tell me what's in your car that those men want so badly? After all, I have a right to know what I risked my life for this morning. Wouldn't you agree?"

"My car? I don't have anything in my car. I just—" Tabitha stopped midsentence. Why was she explaining herself? Just because he helped her didn't mean she had to share her deepest fears with him. They had nothing to do with what had happened today. She took in a deep breath. "Are you interrogating me?"

Rory stretched his neck and glared at the roof of the tent. "Of course not." His voice came out in a growl. "I don't interrogate victims."

"What a relief." She attempted a smile, but it was pointless. The man had transformed into cop mode and apparently wouldn't be satisfied until he'd probed her for answers. Too bad she had none. She chewed on her bottom lip.

Rory rubbed his eyes and sighed. "Tabitha, I know you're frightened. More so than you're letting on and I want to help you. Really, I do. But I can't if you don't tell me what you know."

Pressing her lips together, Tabitha inhaled slowly, determined to answer him with a steady voice. "I promise you I don't know what's going on. I have no idea what those men are after. If I did, I would tell you. I'm just praying my way through this. Otherwise I'm sure I'd be completely hysterical by now."

His brow lifted. "I saw Hines's note about someone named Max. Is he involved in this?"

Tabitha frowned. She didn't like the hint of suspicion in his tone. Did he really think she had something to hide? "Is this what you do as a federal officer? Intimidate people who are scared? I'm not impressed."

Tears continued to press at the corner of her eyes. She lifted her hand to her forehead to scratch an imaginary itch and shield herself from his hard gaze.

"Look," he said, "I'm trying to help. I'm not intending to upset you. This is what I do. I'm an investigator. Now, tell me about Max B. I read that name in the detective's notes. Is that Bristow? Is that the person you booked a room for? This could be important."

Tabitha narrowed her eyes on him. He'd obviously done more than check her room inside the hotel.

"Come on, Tabitha. Talk to me. Let me help."

"Fine," she mumbled. "Bristow and Max are two different people."

"Okay. Let's start with Max. Who is Max?"

"Max B. is Max Beaumont. My brother." Tabitha glanced down. She did not want to repeat the entire story. But when she looked back at Rory, it was obvious that small dose of information wouldn't hold him. "I thought the men who attacked me mentioned him. But I'm not sure. In fact, the more I think about it, the more ridiculous it seems. I think maybe I imagined it."

Knots tightened in her stomach. Each time she mentioned her brother, she felt more and more like she might be getting him into trouble. But why? No way her brother had anything to do with those thugs on the mountain. That was impossible.

Rory's look softened a bit. "How did they mention him?"

"I don't know. They wanted something from me. Something Max gave me…I think that's what they said." Tabitha put her quivering hand to her temple. "I'm so tired. I know you're trying to help but I already went through this with the detectives."

"I'm sorry." He slid a glass of water across the table. "Here, drink some water. You look pale again."

She took a quick drink while he scratched his head and furrowed his brow. She pushed the glass back.

"Better?" he whispered.

She shrugged, noting his expression had lightened. A slight grin curved his lips upward. He reached over the table and touched her hand softly.

Tabitha gaped. How did he do that? Was it part of the interrogation technique? A method to disarm and relax her? Or did he unknowingly morph from tough cop to charmer? Either way, she didn't like it, especially because it seemed to be working. She pulled her hand away.

"So, Max gave you something?" Rory continued.

"No. That's just it. He didn't."

Rory frowned. "Okay. I know this seems silly, but it might be important. Now Max is your brother so I'm sure he gave you something at some point. How about in the past year? Anything?"

"A root canal," she said drily, pointing at her back tooth.

"Cute."

"You said *anything*. Anyway, it's true. He's a dentist. It was a few weeks ago and that's the last time I saw him."

"How about Christmas and your birthday? Don't you exchange presents?"

Tabitha rolled her eyes. "For my birthday, he gave me a gift certificate to a spa. I used it immediately. For Christmas, an ugly sweater which I exchanged for a handbag. Max got married this year. I haven't really seen much of him lately."

"When was that?"

"The wedding? Two months ago." Her mouth twitched.

"You don't seem happy about that."

She shrugged. "Max is happy. Karin, his wife, has been

hard to get to know. Max and I were really close before. It's an adjustment for me."

Rory licked his lower lip and leaned his large body over his knees. "Tabitha, why did you run back to your car like that?"

A tear dropped to her cheek. Her hand moved quickly to brush it aside. "It was nothing. I just want to go home. I wanted my car to be there so I knew I could get home. I don't like being…trapped."

"Trapped?" Rory sat up straight in his chair and scratched his ear. "Sounds like a story there."

"Not one for today," she said, praying that he'd let it go.

He nodded. His mouth held a gentle smile. "You don't need to worry. We'll get you home."

Tabitha wasn't sure what he meant by *we* but it sounded like more help from him and that she did not want. What if he changed back to supercop? Or worse, charmed her again with those electric eyes? "You know, if I had a phone, I could call a friend to pick me up. That is, if you're finished grilling me."

A full smile covered his face. "I'm finished. For now." He felt around his waistline. "I don't have my phone, either. Here."

Before she could say anything, he'd scooped her up in his arms and was weaving his way through the tables, heading for the inn.

"You don't need to carry me! I'm not paraly—" She swallowed the rest of the word, aware of how close she was to his face and neck. Of the strong masculine scent which emanated there.

"Relax," he said. "You must be the tensest person I've ever met."

*Oh, yeah. Relax. Sure.* Her breath stuck in her throat, her senses on overload.

"Please, put me down," she whispered.

"You can't walk. I'm trying to help."

*I don't want any more help. I want to go home.* Tabitha thought she might burst if she didn't get away from him. New tears flooded the corners of her eyes.

As he turned up the stairs, her head jostled back to his shoulder. "That's it. Just relax," he suggested, his soft breath drifting over her neck. "I've got you."

And with his whisper, her tears won their battle, escaping her eyes, flowing out hard and heavy, in narrow, salty streams all the way to her chin and onto Rory's shirt.

# FOUR

The investigation took up a good part of the afternoon. Detectives Greenwood and Hines agonized over every detail before leaving. Rory appreciated their methodical ways, knowing his father would have been pleased that the department still ran tight.

In the cool air-conditioning of the Birchwood Inn, he sat on one end of a hand-carved bench that he'd pulled near Tabitha. On the other end of the bench, he'd propped her ankle. The flesh around it had turned bluish, but the swelling seemed to have gone down a bit. They sipped cold drinks and ate some of the lemon squares Terri had brought.

Tabitha had long ago arranged her ride home, and the police had no further questions for him. Rory no longer had a reason to stay. Yet he lingered. Nervously, he downed his glass of sweet tea and checked his watch. "I should call Gram." He stood abruptly.

Terri stood with him. "Oh, yeah, Gram. I'll need to change your reservation at Nick's."

"Reservation? What reservation?" Rory swallowed hard.

"Oh." Terri pressed her lips together. "I thought you overheard me earlier."

Rory shrugged, eyes widening.

"Well, Tabitha's roommate can't arrive until ten, so I made a dinner reservation for the two of you at Nick's," his cousin said. "But I forgot about Gram. Anyway, I'll just change it from two to three."

*Thanks, Terri. Talk about putting us on the spot.* Rory glanced at Tabitha, trying to gauge her reaction.

"Oh, wow. That's nice but…" Tabitha shook her head from side to side. "I'm so tired and not the least bit hungry. I'll just rest here and wait for my ride."

"You can't sit here all that time. I won't hear of it," Terri said. "So get whatever you need from our boutique and have a great dinner, all compliments of the Birchwood Inn. It's the least we can do." Terri smiled, turned on her heel and headed to her office without giving either of them a chance to respond.

Tabitha turned to Rory with a sly grin. "She's hard to argue with."

"Yep. Can't get a word in. She's always been like that." He scratched his head. "Hey, I didn't know your ride would take so long. I could have driven you home myself."

Tabitha stiffened. "No. You've already done so much. And forget about dinner. I'm sure you already have plans. So, don't worry about me."

"Actually, the plan was dinner with my grandmother. If you don't join us, I'll have to cancel."

She looked up with a suspicious grin. "Now, that's just silly."

Rory shook his head. "Tabitha, I can't leave you here alone. It might not be safe."

"Nonsense. I'll be fine."

"No can do… And Nick's is a great place. Come on. Have dinner with us." He lowered her foot to the floor and replaced the bench against the wall. Then he stood over her with his arms folded.

"Oh, be serious," she argued. "I can't go. I'm filthy and I don't have anything to wear."

Rory was glad that Terri had already taken care of that problem. He would have never thought of the hotel gift shop.

"Not a good excuse. You have a new hotel room and the gift shop at your disposal." He pointed to the boutique that adjoined the front lobby. "I can see a whole wall of women's clothing from here. Come on. I'll walk you over." He offered her an arm.

"I doubt I'll be good company," she continued as he pulled her up.

"You'll be perfect. It will be the best date you've ever had."

"Date? Your grandmother is coming. It's not a date."

Rory felt her stiffen beside him. "It's just a manner of speaking," he explained, wondering why the reference made her so defensive. Many people would call a lot less than dinner at the town's fanciest restaurant a date.

In the boutique, Tabitha selected a few garments and a pair of flip-flops, then insisted on hobbling up the stairs alone. A half hour later, she returned wearing a cream-colored blouse and a long flowered skirt. Her dark brown hair, still damp, promised long, twisting curls and tumbled softly around her face and over her shoulders.

Rory drank in her beauty, then hurried to help her down the last few steps. "You look lovely."

"Thank you." She pushed back her hair then took his arm. "I wish I felt lovely."

"You're just tired."

"Yes, I am," she agreed. "I'm sure you are, too."

"Not really. Just anxious to get a shower."

Rory helped Tabitha out of the inn and across the lawn to his truck. "Gram's at the cabin. She can keep you company while I change."

Tabitha bit her lower lip. "Do you mind if we not talk about what happened today?"

"Sure," Rory said, giving her a lift into the cab of the truck. They both reached for the safety belt. His hand engulfed hers over the small buckle. Her skin felt warm and smooth under his rough hands.

"I got it," she said, lifting her eyes to his. Her fingers tensed under his.

Rory ignored her stiffness. Keeping his eyes locked on hers, he lifted the belt across her lap and secured it. As he leaned over the seat, the aroma of vanilla filled his senses. His eyes drifted to her soft lips. He swallowed hard and retreated, closing the passenger door with care.

*Wow.*

Tabitha remained silent as he cranked up the engine and headed down the mountain.

"I'm sorry I grilled you earlier. I get carried away with the cop thing sometimes. And you kind of freaked me out when you ran after your car like that."

"I kind of freaked myself out. It's been a bad day. I'm sorry I cried all over your shoulder."

"Not at all. I hear that's what they're for."

Her lips twitched upward but still no smile.

Rory searched for something to say, but Terri was right— he was completely out of practice conversing with the opposite sex. "I hope you're not upset about me dragging you to dinner."

"No. I'm not. I just can't understand why my brother won't answer his phone. I tried him again from the room and still no answer."

"Did you talk to his wife?"

"No. But I spoke with his dental partner. He answered the weekend emergency line."

"Does his partner know where he is?"

"Not exactly." She shook her head. "He just said that Max and Karin are having a romantic getaway and that he'd been instructed not to call them. Must have been last second or my brother would have told me."

Rory could see the disappointment in her face and frowned. He didn't want this to be an uncomfortable evening full of the day's fear and bad memories. "You know, I think I'm a little jealous of Max."

She gave him a strange look.

"I don't have any siblings," he explained. And as the simple statement came out, Rory realized how deeply he felt it. Especially now with his father gone.

"I'm lucky. I have a great family." She smiled.

The brightness of her expression lifted his own spirits. "So it was just the four of you, until your brother married?"

"Yes. My dad's a professor of medieval studies. He travels to Europe every summer for research. Every fourth year, he stays abroad somewhere as a visiting professor. He's at Exeter this year. It's one of the reasons Max and I got to be so close. Every summer we just had each other."

"Sounds interesting. Living abroad."

"It was a nice way to grow up."

"What does your mom do?"

"Mostly keep my dad's head on straight." She turned toward him. "What does yours do?"

Rory let out a sigh. "I never knew my mom. She left when I was young."

Tabitha frowned. "I'm sorry. She must be somewhere regretting that. She missed out on a lot."

Rory, expecting pity, chuckled at her response. "That's exactly what my grandmother says. Just between you and me, I don't think Gram liked my mother too much. Says I was the only thing she ever did right."

"But your dad loved her?"

"Oh, yeah. I think until his last breath he expected her to come back. I hated that he died like that."

"Like what? Hopeful?"

"Is that hope or just a waste?"

"Your dad didn't think his hope was a waste."

"She didn't come back." Rory could hear his own bitterness.

"Doesn't mean she didn't love him…and you."

*What else could it mean?*

As they pulled in front of his cabin, Rory felt a lump forming in his throat. He still found himself expecting James Farrell to be inside when he entered. His stomach churned as he turned into the gravel drive. He parked the truck and walked around to help Tabitha from the cab.

She smiled wide as he opened the door. "Is this your grandmother's home? It's beautiful."

Rory felt his lips curl upward. "Actually, it's mine. My dad and I built it."

Tabitha's face seemed to light up as she scanned over the property. "It's gorgeous. Look at that view. It's better than the inn." She stepped out of the truck, occupied with the panorama of mountains. Clumsily, she landed on her bad ankle and fell into him. Rory encircled his arms about her and held her up.

She blushed. He noticed that, for the first time, her body wasn't rigid against him.

Rory looked into her eyes. An awkward smile covered her expression. Her long brown curls blew with the soft breeze and danced around her face. Rory ached to run his hands through them.

"I promise to pay more attention," she vowed. "I can't keep falling all over you."

Had that been his cue to release her? He found himself not able to. He liked the connection—the feeling that she belonged there. At his cabin. In his arms.

She pulled away, her expression dazed. Rory turned her to the front porch. "Come on. Let's meet Gram. You must be the only person in North Carolina who doesn't know her."

"Shame on you, Rory. You didn't tell me you were bringing a guest to dinner." In designer jeans and a green silk blouse, Gram stood at the door of the cabin with one hand on her hip and the other pointed at her grandson. Her short gray hair bounced with each syllable. A welcoming smile defied her authoritative stance and scolding words.

Rory lowered Gram's finger then leaned in and kissed the top of her head. "Gram, this is Tabitha Beaumont. I met her at the triathlon today. She's coming to dinner with us."

The older woman took a step forward and extended a hand. "Hello, dear. I'm Lilly. Please come in."

"Nice to meet you." Tabitha shook the tall, thin-framed woman's hand, noting her eyes possessed the same rich, blue shade as Rory's.

"Nice to meet you, too," Lilly said. "It's about time my grandson had a date. I just wish he had told me. Mr. Watson asked me to the movies this evening. I should have said yes. Instead, I'm going to ruin your dinner tagging along." She passed another scolding glance at Rory. "Now come on in, dear, and tell me what happened to your ankle."

"Mr. Watson?" Rory interrupted. "That little old man who runs the grocery downtown? You're dating him?" Rory hid his face from his grandmother and winked at Tabitha.

Lilly looked indignant. "Mr. Watson is a fine man and watch yourself—he's the same age as I am." She took Tabitha by the arm and escorted her into the house. "Excuse him. I suppose he's showing off. I don't blame him."

Rory's face turned the color of a ripe McIntosh and Tabitha wondered what shade of red her own must have been. She could feel the heat pulsing in her cheeks.

Gram led her into the kitchen. "Now sit right here while I fix some tea and call Mr. Watson. I'll bet he and I can still make that movie."

"Mrs. Farrell, my being here was completely last second. And I wouldn't have come if I thought I was interrupting your time with your grandson. It's not a date. You really should go with us."

"Not a date?" Lilly repeated and looked with disappointment at Rory.

"I'm not saying another word." Rory held his palms high in the air. "You two beautiful women can decide how many for dinner." He glanced nervously at Tabitha. "If you'll excuse me. My turn to shower."

In the kitchen, Lilly poured herbal tea for two and entertained Tabitha with stories about Rory's mischievous youth. Her voice felt like a balm to Tabitha's tired nerves. For a moment, she forgot the horrors of the day and laughed until her belly ached.

"I can't believe he did that," she said. "I just met your grandson but it's hard to imagine him loading school cubbies with toads. He seems so serious now. So honor bound."

"That he is." Lilly frowned a little. "I'm afraid he may come across a little too serious these days. His father's death has been difficult. He's very angry over it."

"Angry? I thought your son died of cancer, not in the line of duty."

"He did die of cancer. And very quickly. Rory's angry at God. Angry his prayers weren't answered." She patted Tabitha's hand. "But don't you worry. He'll work that out. He's a good man. And I should know. I helped his father raise him."

"Well, he adores you. That's for sure." Tabitha forced a smile, saddened to learn of Rory's anger.

"And I adore him, which is why I refuse to go to dinner with you two." She scooted from the table and snatched the portable phone from the kitchen counter.

"No. Please. You should join us." Tabitha tried to persuade Lilly. But her mind was made up. She would not be a "third wheel," as she kept putting it.

While Gram chatted with Mr. Watson, Tabitha thought about spending the evening alone with Rory. Her shoulders tied into knots. *You can do this, Tabitha. You can have dinner with the man who rescued you. You can. It's not a date.*

"Let's go." Rory's voice boomed into the kitchen.

Tabitha hadn't heard him emerge from the back of the cabin. Turning, she followed the deep sound until she found him standing by the front door, adjusting his shirt collar. He looked amazing. She had thought so at the race, but now clean-shaven, dressed in a pair of slacks and a polo shirt, his sculpted features were even more pronounced. His broad shoulders and the strong line of his jaw had definite movie-star quality.

She pulled away her lingering eyes and edged her way to the foyer. Rory helped her to the truck. His strong hand on her elbow sent a tingle to her very core. Gram rode along with them into town, talking all the way. They dropped her at the theater where Mr. Watson waited. And Tabitha feared that what she'd been reluctant to call a date was turning out to be exactly that.

"Your Gram looks happy with Mr. Watson," she noted.

Rory made a muffled sound and turned the truck into the restaurant parking.

Nick's was a small, elegant bistro. She and Rory occupied a tiny table for two in the back of the dining room and ate some of the most delicious Italian food Tabitha had tasted in a long time.

"I'm eating like a truck driver," she claimed. "Sorry. I didn't realize how hungry I was. It's delicious."

"It is. And I'm glad you're eating. It's good to see you relax. You didn't have anything for lunch."

"Neither did you," she countered.

He leaned closer to her with a cockeyed grin. "You noticed? I'm flattered."

"Really? Flattered by that? You should listen to your grandmother and get out more."

Rory's deep baritone laughter filled the small room. Those hypnotic eyes twinkled at her in the candlelight. His grin spread wide under that slightly crooked and freckled nose—his only imperfection, if she could even call it that.

She felt her throat constricting. So far, the dinner had been casual, friendly-like, without any flirtations. This change made her uncomfortable. Uncomfortable because the change wasn't just from him—she felt it in herself, as well.

She looked away as she wiped her mouth with the cloth napkin. She'd be a big fat liar to tell herself she didn't feel attracted to him. Over the past two years, she'd wondered if she could ever feel like this again. She should have been pleased. Instead, it was completely unnerving. "I like your grandmother," she said. "She's spunky."

"You like my grandmother. Great." He sighed and leaned back in his chair. "She didn't wear you out with all her stories and gossip?"

"You forget. I'm a lawyer. I'm used to lots of talking." Except for tonight, she thought. She looked down at her watch. "Wow. Look at the time. We should probably get back to the inn."

"What about dessert?" He looked hopeful.

"No, thank you."

Rory frowned and placed his napkin beside his plate. He leaned forward with those intense eyes boring into her. "Coffee?"

Tabitha shook her head.

"Are you okay? You look pale again."

"I'm fine." But was she? Why did it feel like the walls were closing in? Must have been the mixture of exhaustion, anxiety and emotion catching up with her again. The sooner she was home the better. Away from Hendersonville, that mountain and Rory Farrell.

As they stood, Rory's phone pulsed at his waist. Tabitha tried to look away as he mumbled in low tones, but her eyes were drawn to him like magnets to steel. He glanced her way as he spoke, his smile fading, and she knew the call was about her. About the attack. The pool of dread began to rise around her again.

Rory snapped his cell shut. "That was Detective Hines on the phone. They found your car."

# FIVE

The police had found her car. Tabitha wondered if it looked like her hotel room. The anxious thought made her body turn rigid. Rory reached for her arm. "I don't need help. My ankle is better." The words came out harsher than she'd meant them.

"Your ankle is better because you've been staying off it." With a tug, he forced her to lean on him.

"Where did they find it?" she asked, as he helped her out of the restaurant and toward his truck.

"Abandoned near Interstate 40 not far from Asheville."

"Well, this is good. Right? That they found it?"

Rory frowned and didn't look at her as they walked toward the truck. "Maybe. It's being towed to a lab. They'll call you about it tomorrow."

"But…" She paused in front of the passenger door. "Why did the police call you?"

"Well, for one, you don't have a phone." He opened the door for her. She took a step into the cab, but Rory held fast to her elbow, turning her to face him. She leaned back against the outside of the truck.

Rory released her arm and gave her a nervous, fleeting smile. "Tabitha, I don't… You're very tense again. I hope you're not angry with me for making you come tonight."

She smiled. "No. You would know if I was angry."

"Yes. I bet I would." His expression lightened. With a hand on the window of the cab, he leaned his weight toward her, lowering his head. "So…you're okay?"

Tabitha swallowed hard. *No, I'm not okay. You make me nervous.* She shrugged and slid away toward the open cab.

"One more question," he stated.

Tabitha glanced back. One look into his piercing eyes and she melted, her breath heavy in her chest. Yes, she was definitely attracted to him.

"I know we just met," he continued. "But are you…" He paused to clear his throat. "Are you seeing anyone? Would you consider going out with me sometime?"

"I'm not great at math," she said, climbing into the truck. "But I think that's two questions."

"Okay. You're right." He leaned against the door. "But maybe you'd be kind enough to answer one of them?"

Tabitha drew in a slow breath. His request was simple and fair. Most women would have been flattered by it. After all, he had no way of knowing her past and the complications it threw into his request. But she did. A date with him meant facing her buried fears. It meant having trust and being honest. And Tabitha didn't know if she could do it. Not now. Not ever.

"My answer to one of the questions is no."

Rory's head titled. "No, you're not dating anyone? Or no, you won't go out with me?"

Tabitha turned to him with a grin. "I'm afraid that's more questions, Agent Farrell."

"So it is." He gave a half laugh then closed the door, shaking his head as he walked to the driver's side.

On the way back to the inn, he let her steer the conversation over a variety of impersonal topics. He couldn't know how much she appreciated that.

Rory knew better than to press Tabitha about seeing him again. It was obvious she was exhausted and emotionally drained. Perhaps he'd only imagined the connection he'd felt with her. Had he become that clueless with women? Probably.

He parked in front of the inn and led Tabitha up the long staircase and into the lobby.

"Tabitha." A tall and thin reddish-blonde jumped forward the second they stepped inside. The woman flung her arms around Tabitha, forcing Rory to step back.

Her roommate from Charlotte. Already arrived. The disappointment that Tabitha would be out of his life in less than five minutes hit him like a concrete block in the chest.

"Oh." The woman made fast, nervous gestures as she spoke. "This must be Agent uh—"

"Rory Farrell." He extended his hand, which she grasped with tremendous strength.

"Sasha Bristow."

Bristow. Rory felt his smile return. The other hotel room had been for her roommate. Not a boyfriend. A little of the pressure lifted from his chest. "Nice to meet you, Ms. Bristow."

"Nice of you to save Tabitha and keep her company until my shift ended." Sasha grinned. "I would have been here for the race, if I hadn't had to work."

There was a particular lilt to her accent. Rory couldn't quite place it. "You're a nurse, right?" he asked.

Sasha nodded.

"Well, I don't have any bags, so let's go," Tabitha said quickly.

"Right. I—uh. I need to…" Sasha eyed the interior.

"Ladies' room is over there." Tabitha pointed to the doors next to the boutique. Sasha spun away.

"She has an interesting accent," Rory said.

"Irish, but it's faded since we met in college."

"Ah."

Silence fell between them. But Rory held her gaze, searching for some sign from her. Some indication that he hadn't imagined what he'd felt earlier. Tabitha gave him nothing but a tired expression.

"I know you have to go. But here." He pulled out his wallet, grabbed a card and placed it in her hand, letting his fingers linger over her palm a little longer than necessary. "This is my cell number. I want you to call me if you have any more trouble. I hope you don't, but I'm going to get your address from Terri and have a Charlotte patrol car drive by your home."

She started to reject his idea.

"Don't say no. I'm going to do it anyway. Just for the next few days… Tabitha, you need to be careful. This may not be the end of those men." He brushed a finger down her cheek and lifted her chin. She pulled away and Rory wanted to kick himself for once again making her uncomfortable. "I'm sorry. I shouldn't—"

"No," she interrupted. "It's just…I can't thank you enough for all you've done. I'm glad God chose you to help me."

"God?" He didn't want to talk about God. He wanted to kiss her. He felt the frown form across his face.

"Yes. God," she said, scrunching up her nose at his doubtful look. "When those men grabbed me, I prayed for God to send someone. And He did. He sent you. And I'm so glad."

Rory looked up at the ceiling and remembered his prayer— his own acknowledgment that God had used him. But he couldn't think on it. Too many unanswered questions, too many doubts, too much pain.

"I'm glad He answered *your* prayer," he mumbled, hoping she couldn't hear the anger laced in his words. He sighed and ran his hand over the top of his head. This was not how he wanted to end the evening. "I'm glad I was there, too. But those men are serious and they might come back. You won't be alone tonight, will you?"

"No, Sasha will be there," she answered.

"Good," he said, but he wanted more. A promise to see her again. But that was something he couldn't have. Tabitha would forever connect him with this terrible day and that was that. He had to back off and forget his attraction to her.

Sasha returned promptly and the two ladies headed out. He tried to help, but Sasha moved beside her friend and took over.

"I got it," she said.

Rory followed them out of the inn, feeling lost and alone. His time of helping Tabitha had ended. As the two women drove away into the darkness, he walked to his truck with his head down. The sound of their car faded into the night and the solitude of the mountain overwhelmed him.

# SIX

"Goodbye, girls. See you next week." Tabitha waved as the last two teenage girls from her Sunday-school class headed to their car.

"Goodbye, Miss Beaumont. Thanks for the pizza." They hopped inside the compact, revved the engine, then wove a bit recklessly through the busy parking lot of Joe's Pizzeria.

Tabitha held her breath. *Lord, please keep them safe.*

Earlier that morning, she had been ready to dismiss her usual Sunday-morning routine and stay in bed. But she remembered her promise to take the girls to lunch after the Sunday service. She smiled inwardly, knowing the sacrifice of a few hours' sleep had been well worth the fellowship. Fellowship she'd needed as well as provided.

But now Tabitha stood alone on the sidewalk. Her intention had not been to be the last one at the restaurant, but the lunch hadn't taken as long as she'd planned. She had half a notion to run after the girls and ask for a ride. No. She was being silly. She had to get over what had happened on the mountain yesterday. Put it behind her.

Clutching her purse under her arm, she checked her watch. Sasha would be along soon. Still, a feeling of helplessness washed over her. She hated not having a car or a cell phone.

A small green sedan pulled into the parking lot and Tabitha backed away from the curb as it passed. She told herself not to be so edgy, but for the next ten minutes, each time a car passed or pulled in, she flinched. Every time a patron exited the restaurant, she skittered.

She remembered Rory's warning for her not to be alone. But he'd meant at home. Right?

She checked her watch again. Sasha was late. She pulled nervously at a lock of her hair. Could her friend have forgotten? She didn't see how. They'd just seen each other at church. Sasha had said she had a few errands to run. Then she was going to join them at the restaurant. So, where was she? Sasha was never late.

Tabitha shook her head at her nervous thoughts. What could happen to her in broad daylight, two feet from the front door of a crowded restaurant?

Nothing.

And still, she couldn't shake the strong feeling of unease.

After a few minutes, a large black SUV with tinted windows pulled into the parking lot and with it a deeper apprehension consumed her. Again, she backed away from the curb. The car circled the lot and Tabitha was sure she sensed the driver's eyes on her. Her tired mind was imagining things. She couldn't see a thing through the dark glass. But no matter the logic she sought, her panic continued to grow.

The vehicle circled the entire building—a strange thing to do, since there were plenty of empty parking spots in front. Again, Tabitha told herself she was overreacting.

*Get inside.* The command whispered through her mind and Tabitha heeded. She strode back into the restaurant at breakneck speed. From the windows, she watched the SUV pull to where she had stood at the curb.

No one got out. No one got in.

And she still felt that someone inside the vehicle was watching her. This time, she was sure of it. Tabitha began to shake from head to toe.

Several minutes passed and the big black vehicle finally

moved on, turning out of the parking lot just as Sasha's red MINI Cooper pulled into its place. On weak legs, Tabitha hobbled to the car, jumped in and slammed the door.

"Sorry I'm late. The checkout lines at the mart were heinous." Sasha glanced over. "Japers! You should have stayed in bed, girl. You look worse than me dead uncle."

"Thanks."

"No, really. You look terrible bad. Should I fetch you a doctor?"

"No. I ate too much pizza. That's all." Tabitha clutched at her purse to steady her quivering fingers.

"Right. What really happened?" Sasha asked.

"I got spooked. That's all." Tabitha took a deep breath and swallowed hard. "I hate not having a car or a phone. I hate all of this. It's like—"

"Now, don't get started on all that." Sasha patted her arm as she drove away from the restaurant. "I know just what you need."

"Really? Enlighten me."

"You need a rental car. How does that sound?"

"Yes. That is a good idea." Tabitha nodded.

"We'll head out right now to pick one up and on the way, you can tell me all about that spicy agent." Her roommate grinned. "I tried to ask you last night but you fell asleep before we got to the highway."

Tabitha pretended not to hear. She didn't want to talk about Rory. It was bad enough she couldn't stop thinking about him on her own. "You know, I have a big deposition tomorrow. Once we get a car, I'll have to head home to get prepared. What are you doing this afternoon?"

"Oh. So, it's like that, is it?" Sasha smirked.

"Like what?"

"If you weren't interested, you'd say so. You have eyes for him. O' course, who wouldn't?"

Tabitha folded her arms across her chest. "I don't know what you're talking about."

Sasha raised an eyebrow at her.

Tabitha dropped her arms to her lap. "I don't have 'eyes for him,' as you put it. He just helped me. That's all."

"Uh-huh," Sasha said doubtfully. "Just helped ya."

"Look. I don't want to talk about any part of yesterday. Okay?" She sighed. She didn't like shutting Sasha out. But what good would it do to talk about Rory Farrell? She wasn't going to see him again. She'd made that decision last night.

Conversation over, Tabitha reached for the air vent, turning it so that the flow blew directly onto her face. The sleeve of her long blouse meant to cover the red marks on her wrists rode up, exposing her battered arms.

"Good gracious!" Sasha gasped. "I was wondering why you were wearing that blouse in this heat."

Sasha grabbed Tabitha's other arm and drew back the sleeve. Deep purple bruises and red skin burns encircled her wrist.

"Those men did that to you?" Sasha could barely get the question out. "What else did they do? They didn't… It wasn't like last time, was it?"

"No. No." Tabitha felt her eyes fill with tears. "That's all they did. Nothing else. Thanks to God." And Rory.

After preparing her deposition, Tabitha cooked dinner for Sasha and herself. Grilled steaks and veggies. She'd even eaten some. Placing the last of the dishes into the washer, she tried to settle her mind, still buzzing with thoughts of yesterday's attack. It was late, though. And while she was tired, she knew that sleep would be a long way off. The phone rang as she wiped the countertop. She picked it up and watched her brother's name roll across the caller ID window. A sudden sense of hope raced through her veins.

"Max! Where have you been all weekend?"

"Karin and I drove to Annapolis," he said as if repeating himself for the tenth time. "I left you four messages, Tabs. You should check your cell once in a while."

She sucked in her breath. Of course, her brother had tried to call her. "It's hard to check something you don't have."

"What do you mean?"

"My phone, my car, everything I took to Hendersonville was stolen."

"You're kidding!"

"I wish I were." Without skipping a detail, Tabitha described the attack and events that followed. Afterward, a curious silence followed.

Tabitha held the phone close to her ear and hobbled from the tiny kitchen into the more spacious den, where Sasha sat sprawled over a worn leather chair watching the evening news. Tabitha tucked herself into a corner of the chenille couch. Sasha glanced over, knowing how anxious she'd been to talk to her brother. Max hadn't spoken so Tabitha merely shrugged, his prolonged silence frustrating her more by the second. "Max, are you there?" she asked impatiently.

"Ye-yeah," he said. "Of course. Sorry. I was just thinking that I should have gone with you. We could have raced together. And I…" He mumbled more regrets that became less and less audible.

Tabitha dropped her face into the palm of her hand. This was not the response she'd anticipated. In fact, tonight Max's attitude had none of the usual intensity. He hadn't even commented about the attackers mentioning his name, nor did he laugh and proclaim that he'd never given her anything. Fear gripped her. The hope she'd held on to, that Max could assuage her anxieties, was slipping away. "What's wrong? What's going on?" she demanded.

"What? Nothing—" Max cleared his throat. "Nothing's going on, I was just trying to think it through, you know. Why in the world would they have used my name like that? But really, I have no idea." He paused again. "Tabitha, you know I had nothing to do with it, right?"

Her heart sank to the pit of her stomach. This was not Max. Sure, she heard her brother talking, but this wasn't the person she knew and loved. Tabitha rubbed her fingers against her temple and fought the urge to scream at the top of her lungs. Had his marriage caused this change? Or was it her imagination that she felt distanced from him?

She sighed. "Of course, I don't think you had anything to do with those criminals." *Maybe?* "One of the investigators said they might have used your name to gain false trust. So that I would go with them more easily."

"Well, I'm glad you didn't. But, Tabs, that would mean they know a lot about you. That's unnerving. What else did the police say?"

"Not much. But they're doing a thorough investigation. I'm surprised they haven't called you."

"They may have—Paul said I had several messages. Yours was the first. So, Tabs, why didn't you have Paul contact me? You should have called me immediately."

"I tried. Paul said you didn't want to be disturbed. He said he had no way to reach you."

Max was silent for another moment. "Look, Tabitha. I'm going to come down and stay with you for a few days."

"No, Max. Don't," she said, although his offer did much to soften her frustration. "It's not necessary. Sasha is with me. I'm fine. The police are driving by every hour. Anyone would be crazy to try to get in here."

"And your security system?"

"On 24/7."

"Don't you think it would be better if I was there?" Max began to talk faster and faster. "Yeah. I'm going to come down. If I leave now, I can be there by midnight. And tomorrow, we'll get you a big, mean dog, like a Doberman or a mastiff."

Tabitha smiled. Now Max sounded like her hyper, overprotective brother. It filled her with a sense of warmth. "I'm not discussing this with you. You're not coming down."

"I want to, Tabs. I can easily reschedule my patients for the next few days. It's no big deal. Karin won't mind."

Tabitha wasn't so sure. Her relationship with her sister-in-law was strained at best. This might make it worse. Anyway, tomorrow she'd be back at work, in court most of the week. She didn't need Max for that. It would be silly and selfish to have him drive or fly down.

"I'm sure Karin doesn't want you to leave. You're still newlyweds."

"No. Really," Max said. "She just got this little puppy from the SPCA. She's spending every second with it. She won't even notice I'm gone."

"Really, you guys got a dog?"

"Yes, he's adorable. We named him Hoover because he walks around, licking the floors all the time," Max elaborated. "Let me come down, Tabs. We'll get you a dog, too. One you can run with."

"No, Max. I don't need a dog. And don't come. I have a crazy schedule this week. I'd hardly know you were here."

They argued for a few minutes longer until Max finally quit pushing the issue. He began inquiring about the earlier part of her triathlon. She asked him about his weekend in Annapolis. Slowly, the conversation became more relaxed, more normal. At least, as normal as it had been since Max had married Karin.

Twenty minutes later, she hung up, not at all certain she felt better than before he had called.

# SEVEN

Monday afternoon, Rory entered the Charlotte FBI Field Office. Special Agent in Charge Pat Hausser welcomed him into his small corner office.

"Captain Farrell. Or, Agent Farrell," Hausser corrected. "Good to see you again."

Rory took the SAC's hand in a firm shake, remembering well several risky missions his marine unit had conducted for the man in order to bring him terrorist intelligence.

"I'm glad you came in, son," Hausser said. "I'm tired of you turning down my job offers. Now that you're here, I hope you'll take me seriously."

Rory smiled. "I take everything you say seriously, sir. But I thought our meeting today was about a cold case."

"Forget the cold case for now—I'll have someone go over it with you in a minute. Have a seat, son." Hausser motioned to a chair, then positioned himself behind his own desk. "I'm forming a special urban terrorist unit. I need you to lead it. You've been bred for this. You'd be based here in Charlotte but involved in some serious travel. And I know how you marines like to travel."

"Thank you for considering me. It's an interesting offer."

Hausser's smile faded. The man leaned over his desk and clasped his fingers together over a large pile of papers. "You still don't want to leave NCIS?"

"Actually, moving a little closer to my family has great appeal." Not to mention, he knew a nice lawyer in town that he wouldn't mind bumping into. Rory looked down at the gray berber carpet and scratched behind his neck. "But switching agencies? I don't know. I like where I am. I love my team."

Hausser leaned back against his big leather chair and let out a long sigh. "Are you listening? This would be your own team. And there's one more carrot to throw."

Rory lifted his head.

"Word is that Fenton's back in the States. It would be your first case." The words put a grin to Hausser's lips.

"Is that so?" Rory tried to sound calm, but the possibility of leading a team against one of the world's most notorious illegal arms dealers was more than interesting. It was downright tempting.

Hausser lifted a large folder. "I've got the file right here—all ready for you to look over."

Rory rubbed a hand over his mouth then shook his head. "I don't know, sir."

"Well, don't answer yet. Think it through. It would be a huge career step. Not to mention if you take the job, then I can finally say we're even. I'm sick of owing you a favor."

"You don't owe me, sir. I was just doing my job."

"Pulling me out of a burning van was not part of your job that day."

Rory grinned. "It seemed to find its way into my schedule."

"So it did." Hausser nodded. "Well, Farrell, I've got a situation on my hands. I'm going to have to cut this short and turn you over to Jones for that cold case debriefing." The SAC stood. "I can tell you have some things to think over. But the offer for the task team stands. Take two weeks to consider."

"I will. Thank you." They shook hands. An hour later, Hausser's serious expression lingered in Rory's mind as he left the field office. Was this what he needed? His own task unit? Would a change of venue appease the anger in his heart?

He knew it wouldn't.

The late-afternoon heat seared the downtown streets of Charlotte. Rory climbed into his Dodge Ram. He should get on the road and head to Virginia. But he didn't.

Instead, he cranked the HEMI-V8 engine and followed the MapQuest route to Tabitha Beaumont's home—not really certain why he needed to see her. When she'd left Hendersonville two days before, he'd truly believed he'd be able to dismiss the way he'd felt around her. He had his own issues to resolve without adding her into the mix. But she'd been constantly in his thoughts.

The previous night, he'd walked the long wooden porch of his mountain cabin wishing for an excuse, for some reason to visit—like returning her stolen things or bringing her news of the investigation. But he had nothing, until early today when the call had come to bring him to Charlotte. He just wanted to see her. He wondered if she'd feel the same.

After sitting for twenty minutes in congested downtown traffic, he found her small brick rancher. He smiled at its neat, attractive appearance. Not wanting to block the roommate's car in her driveway, he parked down the street. He stepped out of his truck and the August heat stole his breath and his courage. Instead of going to her door, he circled the vehicle, pausing to consider the pros and cons of an unannounced visit.

In contrast to the turbulent weekend, Monday passed without incident for Tabitha. Evidence reviewed in the deposition had forced the opposing party to settle. Her ankle felt better. At lunch, she'd fit in an upper-body workout at the pool—sixty laps of all arms freestyle. Enough to ensure a good night's sleep.

She pulled her rental sedan into her narrow driveway behind Sasha's compact, wondering why her housemate's car was still there. Sasha had said earlier that she'd been called in for a shift at the hospital. Then again, her E.R. schedule changed frequently and without much notice.

Tabitha slipped off her uncomfortable dress shoes, grabbed her leather case from the backseat and rambled barefoot along her front walk. She inspected the flower beds flanking each side and waved at some neighbors as they passed. The sun was still high and the air warm; she breathed in the moist heat.

Her yard was tiny, just some patches of grass and a few small planting areas. But she'd worked hard to keep everything pruned and healthy. Despite the recent lack of rain, all looked well—the only exception, a droopy hydrangea, hanging low in the sweltering afternoon heat. She could sympathize. She felt a little wilted herself in the thick humidity with her skirt and blouse clinging to her damp skin. She couldn't wait to exchange the ensemble for a pair of baggy shorts and a tank top.

"Tabitha?"

The deep voice caused her to jump. But then she recognized its warm tone. She turned and now saw the large truck across the street. Having come in from the other direction, she'd missed it and Rory Farrell. "Was I expecting you?"

"No." He smiled, crossed the street and stepped into her yard. "I had an appointment in town. I thought I'd check on you. I hadn't heard anything."

She smiled back, confirming the blue of his eyes to be just as intense as she'd remembered. "Well, you know what they say about 'no news is good news.'"

He nodded, strolling closer and closer. His eyes fixed on her. His tight black T-shirt stretched across his chest and was tucked into a pair of khaki-colored slacks. Cowboy boots underneath. He looked perfect, until she noticed the bruising under his eyes and across his cheeks.

"You *did* break your nose, didn't you?"

"It's been broken before, often enough for me to know that it can't be reset for a few more days." A step from her now, he tilted his head and took a lock of her loose hair. He twirled the curl between his fingers. "Is this how you dress for work?"

Feeling the heat rise in her cheeks, Tabitha glanced down. She checked her professional attire, then frowned at him for asking such a strange question. "Yes. Conservative. Part of the job." She held up her shoes. "These are usually on my feet."

His face remained expressionless as he gave a single nod and released her tress of hair. "Hmm. How's the ankle?"

"Better. Better than your nose."

"Part of the job," he said, slowly shaking his head. Then he released a low whistle between his teeth. "Every time I see you, you look more and more amazing."

"Thank you. But look at you," she said, gesturing to his nice clothing. "No blood, no running shoes. Oh, but the haircut. That gives you away."

They smiled awkwardly at each other. Tabitha had trouble swallowing.

"I hope you don't mind that I stopped by," he offered.

"Of course not. I hope you weren't waiting long."

"No. Just arrived. I'd hoped to bring some news of the investigation, but there isn't any."

"I know." Tabitha glanced down at the walkway. "I talked to Detective Greenwood at lunch."

Taking one final step to meet her toe-to-toe, Rory leaned over for her briefcase. One by one, his fingers replaced each of hers until he'd relieved her of the leather bag. Tabitha meant to back away, but she seemed cemented to her spot.

"I'm on my way home," he explained. "To work…to Alexandria. But I was hoping you'd accept an invitation to dinner with me first."

"Tonight?" She looked up fast.

"Yes. Right now."

"Oh. Well. I—I have to…uh—" Tabitha stuttered, trying to come up with an excuse. Another dinner with Rory was not a good idea.

Rory frowned. "So, it was yes, you're dating someone? And no, you won't go out with me?"

Tabitha sighed. As tempting as it was, she wasn't going to lie. "No. I answered your first question."

"Good," he said, moving his head quickly down to hers. His warm lips brushed across her own.

Tabitha closed her eyes. His touch was so soft and pleasing. It took all of her will to step back. "That. We shouldn't do that."

Rory looked dazed. "I can't think of a single reason why not," he countered, grabbing her hand. "I couldn't stop thinking about you, Tabitha. Please say you'll go to dinner with me."

Dinner? Who was thinking about dinner? Her mind was reeling from that kiss. How did he do it? Why didn't she flinch and recoil like the last time someone had tried to kiss her? It hadn't been that long ago—she'd thought she was ready to date again. But she'd been wrong. The experience had brought back every bad feeling. The anxiety. The guilt. Endless self-doubt.

She wouldn't risk it again. Not even with Rory Farrell. She hardly knew him. She was crazy to even consider it.

Tabitha shook her head and took another step toward the front door. "I can't go to dinner, but come in. I'll fix you some coffee."

Rory followed her under the covered porch, holding her bag. She fiddled with the key to the dead bolt, but as it turned out, she didn't need it. The door wasn't locked.

It swung open and Tabitha froze at what lay before her. Toppled furniture, emptied drawers and broken glass spread everywhere. Her entire den destroyed.

"Sasha!" Tabitha gasped. "Oh, Lord, please let her be safe."

She made a move into the house, but Rory grabbed her at the elbow and pulled her back. He moved her against the outside wall. With one hand, he retrieved the firearm tucked into his waist. With the other, he gave her the cell from his belt clip. "Call the police," he instructed. He turned to move inside.

"No." She clenched his arm desperately. "Please let me go with you. She's my best friend."

Rory gave her a disapproving look but stood beside her

against the outer wall and dialed Emergency. Then, taking her by the arm, he led her through the disaster that was her home.

"Stay close," he ordered.

She did. She held on to the back of his shirt as they made their way with slow steps through the rubble of the den and dining area. Her eyes filled with tears from fear and worry of what they might find.

Sasha.

She prayed silently and maybe sometimes aloud for her feisty Irish friend. Tabitha could never live with herself if something had happened to Sasha—not in her house.

After passing through the kitchen, they crept down the single hall to the bedrooms. A faint knocking sounded from the bathroom. Rory moved fast, gun ready. He swung the door open and stepped in.

Tabitha couldn't see around him but when he relaxed and put his gun away, she pushed past him and gasped. Sasha lay on the hard tiled floor, gagged and handcuffed to the toilet base. But she was alive and awake and alert.

"Oh, thank You. Thank You, God." Tabitha pulled the tape from her mouth and put her hands on her friend's cheeks. "I'm so sorry."

"I need water," Sasha said with a hoarse voice, tears filling her eyes.

Tabitha moved to get her a drink, fighting her own tears. "Let Rory get you out of those cuffs."

"They left you a message." Sasha's voice croaked.

"Yes, they did." Rory pointed to the mirror over the sink where, with a bar of Dove, someone had written:

> YOU
> BULLET
> MAX

# EIGHT

Authorized vehicles of all shapes and sizes lined the street in front of Tabitha's red brick rancher. Lights flashed. Radios squawked. Uniformed and plainclothes law enforcement personnel hustled to work the scene. Tabitha took little notice. Her only concern was Sasha. Those men from the mountain had found her home—*ruined* her home—and hurt her friend. The note they'd left had her trembling, wondering if she would ever feel safe again.

Holding Sasha's hand, she stood silently as the paramedics worked on her. It was obvious Sasha's Irish accent and willowy good looks had sparked their interests. Tabitha clenched her teeth as they bombarded Sasha with personal questions that had nothing to do with her health.

"Mild concussion," one of them said at length. "But I think you're over the worst of it. Are you up to answering some questions?"

Tabitha gawked. Isn't that what the poor woman had been doing for the past thirty minutes? "Don't you think she should go to the hospital?" Tabitha asked, the edginess sounding in her voice.

The EMT glanced at Tabitha, then turned to Sasha and smiled. "No. Like I said, there's no need, unless you're experiencing nausea or double vision."

Sasha looked at Tabitha. "See? I'm fine. So, let's get these questions done."

"There's the guy you need to see." The EMT pointed to a stocky man standing near Rory's truck, who waved them over as soon as they looked his way.

"I'm Detective Marks from the Charlotte PD. I need to take statements from both of you." He pulled down the tailgate of the truck. "Agent Farrell said we could sit here since things are a little messy inside."

*A little messy?* Ha. Understatement of the century. Her home was a wreck. Tabitha frowned at the reminder. "Where is Agent Farrell?" she said to herself more than to the others.

"Yes. Where is Agent Farrell?" Sasha repeated loudly while jabbing Tabitha with her elbow.

Tabitha ignored her, hoping Detective Marks hadn't noticed the childish exchange.

"He's inside with two FBI agents." The detective tugged on his belt. "They're concerned about the message and the attempted abduction over the weekend and we often work cases like this with the FBI. But I'll be investigating the break-in. So, if you're ready, I have some questions."

While Sasha talked to Detective Marks, Tabitha's mind shot from one horror to the next—the attack on the mountain, her wrecked home, the crazy message, Sasha tied up, her previous assault. She tried to push the images from her mind, but couldn't. Prayer could fix that. *With Him, I can endure all things....*

Tabitha thanked God for keeping Sasha safe and sending Rory her way once again. Pressing her thoughts to the Lord, some relief came to her nervous mind as Sasha continued to talk about the break-in.

"I'd just come back from a run," Sasha explained for the third time. Her accent, as was always the case when she was stressed or upset, rolled out thick and undulating. "I was resetting the security system. He? She? They? I don't know, must have come in and hit me here." She pointed to the back of her neck. "I don't remember a thing after that. I never saw or heard them. Later I woke up on the floor, under the Jacks, handcuffed and all that."

"The Jacks?" the detective repeated.

"The potty," she clarified.

"Ah." Detective Marks nodded then shifted his questions to Tabitha. He didn't appear convinced that she had no notion of what the word *bullet* written on the mirror meant. He asked her if she'd heard from Max. She told him that she hadn't, not since Sunday night.

By the time the detective had finished, Tabitha was hot, tired and tied in knots. She put her arm around Sasha's shoulder. "I'm so sorry. What happened to you is all my fault."

"Not at all." Sasha squeezed her hand. "I'm glad it was me. You, they would have taken."

Tabitha leaned into her. "Thanks. You're a true friend. Let's just hope they found what they wanted or have finally seen that I don't have it…whatever 'it' is."

"Tabitha," Sasha said in a whisper, "you know as well as I do, if they'd found what they were looking for, they wouldn't have left a threatening message. We can be brave, but let's not be foolish."

Tabitha closed her eyes. She hated the helplessness. Not knowing why these people were after her. Thinking of what they'd done to her roommate. And her brother? How was Max involved? How *could* he be involved?

A wave of dizziness made her stomach roll. "I need to move. Walk around or something," she stated.

"Don't go far," Sasha admonished.

Staring down at the sidewalk, Tabitha moved away. If she could just step into the next yard…put the sounds of the crime scene behind her. Maybe she could settle her nerves a bit, but two quick steps placed her right into a very solid body.

"Easy there," Rory said, backing her out of his chest.

She thought about scooting around him. But before she could, he placed a hand on her lower back and guided her to a corner of her lawn. Far enough from the others to give them some privacy. Not far enough that Tabitha could put the scene from her mind.

Rory ran a hand through his short hair. His jaw was clenched tight. He didn't look happy. "Why didn't you tell me that you had talked to your brother?"

She shrugged. "What? I was supposed to call you and tell you that?"

"No. I guess not. But today, when I arrived, you might have mentioned it."

"When? When you were asking me to dinner?" Tabitha smirked.

Rory rubbed his eyes as if he had a sudden headache. The phone at his hip vibrated. With an aggravated grunt, he pulled it from the clip and read the display. "Sorry. I have to take this."

She nodded, glad for the interruption. The man made her crazy. Did he want a date or did he want to scold her? She couldn't keep up.

Rory put the phone to his ear and turned away. Tabitha tried to compose herself, put some sense into her spinning thoughts. This thing with Rory, whatever it was, wasn't important. The only thing that mattered right now was finding a way to shake the crazy people after Max and her.

After his quick phone call, Rory replaced his cell to his clip and looked at her. She didn't wait for him to talk.

"I understand you brought the FBI here?" she asked.

"Yes." He nodded. "I have a friend at the Bureau."

"Of course you do." She relaxed her stance a bit and glanced at her hands. "Rory, I would have told you about Max's call over coffee. We just didn't get that far."

"How was your brother?"

Tabitha pushed a loose strand of hair behind her ear. "I think he was as surprised as anyone about what happened in Hendersonville." Or was he? Perhaps Max had seemed more worried than surprised. Maybe that's what had unnerved her so.

Rory paused. "Well, anything he knows could be helpful. This situation…" He reached out, placing his palm against her cheek. "It's not good. It's escalating and that's got me more than concerned."

Tabitha felt the warmth of his hand against her skin. Her eyes grazed over his lips and she remembered his soft kiss. She pressed her hand to his then pulled it away from her cheek. Their fingers intertwined then broke apart. Already, she missed the contact. "So, what do you 'big agents' think? Should I go into hiding?"

"Would you consider it?"

"No." She folded her arms over her chest.

"I didn't think so." Rory's gaze traveled to Sasha sitting in the back of his truck then again to her. "Tabitha, that was my boss. I'm needed for a case. I have to go. But please be smart. You need help and protection. Don't refuse anything the PD offers you. These are good people. Listen to them and do whatever they suggest."

Tabitha looked down. She wished he weren't leaving. Whether she understood it or not, he made her feel protected.

"Do you have a safe place to go tonight?"

"Sasha's half brother lives in Huntersville. It's just north of here. But he has a family. I don't want to put them in danger."

"Half brother?" he asked. "Different last name?"

"Yes. Sasha uses her mother's name."

"I think that should be good for tonight." Rory chewed his lower lip for a second. "I might be tied up for a few days. But call me anytime. I mean that. I…I really have to go. You have my card, right?" He began to move away.

She nodded. "Rory? Thanks. Again." Like a desperate child she grabbed his hand as he passed. "And about dinner? Maybe it wasn't such a bad idea. I mean, I could take you out sometime. You know, as a thank-you for all your help."

One side of Rory's mouth curled upward. "I've never let a woman pay for my dinner, but if that's the only way you'll go out with me, I'm willing to give it a try."

"Not a date. Just a thank-you dinner," she said, trying not to sound uncomfortable.

"Right. Not a date." He leaned his head toward her and whispered in her ear. "Call it whatever you want. For me, it will be a date."

Heat rose up her neck. "But—"

He briefly put his free hand to her lips. "Call me if you need help. Call me anyway." Dropping her hand, he stepped away. "I really have to go."

Not wanting to watch him leave, Tabitha turned her back to his truck. She walked slowly to the front door of her home and surveyed the damage in her den.

*Why, Lord? Why is this happening?*

# NINE

Finally. The exit to Reston. The six-hour drive to Northern Virginia had been painfully slow for Rory, his mind muddled and serious. He hated not being there during the initial investigation. That put him behind, which meant a very long night.

And work wasn't the only thing on Rory's mind. Seeing Tabitha again had affected him more than he cared to admit. When she'd uttered those soft prayers as they searched for her friend, showing such brave disregard for her trashed home, he had witnessed for a second time the quality woman that she was.

He couldn't shake the image of her in that simple skirt and blouse, standing barefoot on her front walk. It amazed him how unaware of her own beauty she was. Not just her outward beauty. Rory had met plenty of pretty women in his life. It was who Tabitha was on the inside that intrigued him, fascinated him and made him want to know her more.

He hoped the Charlotte police would keep her safe. It was clear somebody wanted something from her and they were pretty serious about getting it. But who and what? The vague message on the mirror hadn't really helped except to confirm that her brother was connected to the affair. If Rory could find any free time in the next few days, he would conduct some research on Dr. Max Beaumont. He wanted Tabitha safe. And the sooner she was, the sooner he could have dinner with her. That idea made him warm all over.

Reaching for his cell, Rory placed another call to the Charlotte PD. It took five minutes to get through to Detective Marks, but he learned that Tabitha was tucked away at the home of her friend's brother with a patrol car outside. The news didn't stop him from thinking about her, but it did ease his worries a little.

A very little.

An NCIS van sat in front of the large corner unit where his boss had directed him. Rory parked and walked toward the dwelling. His investigative team passed him on the sidewalk.

"You're late, Farrell," one of them teased him.

"You guys already finished?" Rory asked.

"Yeah, man. The ME took the body an hour ago. Nobody inside now but Stroop. He's waiting for you."

Rory turned back with a smirk. "I'm not worried. Technically I'm still on vacation."

They laughed and waved at him as they pulled away.

Rory headed into the condo then let out a whistle. The place was nothing less than spectacular, spacious and full of lavish decor. Plush chocolate-colored suede sofas and hard dark woods he couldn't help but admire. A cathedral ceiling filled with soft recessed lights pulled the eye to the massive media system and an enormous stone hearth, and showcased several bright oil canvases.

Rory didn't know much about art, but the huge paintings, obviously part of a series, looked impressive and expensive. One seemed to be missing, he thought, staring at an empty portion of wall.

"Farrell." Special Agent Stroop called him over. His thin, gray-headed boss leaned against a granite countertop in the kitchen. For a brief second, a smile replaced his normally somber and indifferent expression. "Nothing like getting right back to work after vacation, huh? Sorry to rush you, but this couldn't wait."

They shook hands with a firm grip. "Good to be back, sir. What did I miss?"

Stroop motioned for Rory to follow him into another room,

a large office. He pointed to a computer desk where a small circle of blood had pooled. Some spatter fanned out and covered part of the wall to the right. "Thirty-six-year-old, naval research scientist R. T. Henly, nanotech specialist. Single gunshot to the head."

"Nanotech?" Rory repeated. "That's some weird stuff. I read an article about it in *The Post*. About these microscopic robots you swallow in a capsule. Once they're inside, they're programmed to work on your body like little surgeons. Pretty wild, huh?"

"Yeah, wild," Stroop said with little enthusiasm.

Rory studied the chalk outline where the body had been and the surrounding blood spatter. "I'd say shot at close range. Almost like he did it himself."

His boss expelled a lazy chuckle. "It was staged like a suicide. The murder weapon was even found in his hand. But Henly didn't pull the trigger. There was no shot residue on the victim's hand. The gun was placed in his right and Henly's a southpaw. There was no note. The weapon was a 9 mm with a filed-off serial number—not exactly something a reputed scientist would have on hand. Not to mention, we found a registered Walther packed away in his desk. We also noted many items *possibly* missing from the home."

*A robbery gone bad?* Rory inspected the wood shelves behind the desk. He spotted a snapshot of a man in his middle to late thirties positioned behind the wheel of a large sailing vessel. He had dark curly hair with thick matching eyebrows. The tiny eyes and chemically enhanced smile against his large frame gave Rory the creeps.

"This Henly?" He pointed to the photo.

"Yep," Stroop affirmed. "Looks more like an overgrown frat boy than a scientist. Hard to believe he headed up a division at the Office of Naval Research. New weaponry. Highly classified. Apparently, he was a genius."

"Ah." Rory nodded as a connection clicked in place.

"Weapons." Anderson Fenton, the arms dealer Hausser had baited him with, came to mind. "I saw Hausser in Charlotte."

"Still trying to woo you to the FBI?"

Rory tilted his head in a noncommittal fashion. "He said Fenton is back. Is that true?"

"I haven't heard that." Stroop looked around the room. "I'll mention it to the Secretary."

"Yes. Experimental weapons. The Secretary of Defense must be all over this." Rory replaced the photo to its shelf and continued searching through the victim's books and folders.

Stroop grunted in agreement.

"So, who would want to kill Dr. Henly, nanotech engineer?" Rory mumbled to himself. He scanned the room. "Where's his computer?"

"Com-pu-*ters*. Plural. Agent Jameson took them to the lab, along with his cell, PDA and all those other things people have nowadays."

Rory headed to the next set of shelves. "TOD?"

"Body temp gave us around 5:00 p.m."

"Who found him?"

"Dr. Lee Kim, an old friend from grad school. Works at the Smithsonian. Claims he and Henly planned to get drinks at Steinman's happy hour. Said they do every Monday night. When Henly didn't answer the door or his phone, Dr. Kim unlocked the front door with a key Henly kept out front for emergencies. Henly had been dead an hour or so. We've already confirmed the story."

Rory continued his survey of the room. Besides computers, it didn't seem as if much was missing. "Did Dr. Kim notice anything missing?"

"Kim said that Henly carried one of those USB storage devices with him at all times. A 'data stick' he called it? Anyway, there was nothing like that on him tonight, nor in the house. Not in his car, either."

"Anyone see there's a painting missing in the living room?"

"Dr. Kim did. I have an agent looking into it. Perhaps Henly was living a little beyond his means. His records don't indicate that he came from money, so unless government scientists are getting paid a lot more than they used to, Henly had some supplemental income."

Rory moved to study a set of plaques and trophies on display in a sizable glass encasement. "Anything else we know about Henly? Family trouble? Gambling? Drugs?"

"Not so far. Then again…that would be your job, Farrell."

He cocked a half smile at Stroop. "Just trying to catch up."

"All I can tell you is that according to his FBI file, he's squeaky clean."

Rory gave his boss a knowing look.

"Actually," Stroop continued, "Henly's work is so classified I had a hard time getting an agent into his lab. Really, all we know is that he attended MIT and Hopkins, graduating at the top of his class. Looks like he studied in Europe at some point." He pointed to a diploma from the University of Zurich hanging on the other side of the room. "His parents are retired, in Naples, Florida. He has one brother. Older. Married and living in Chicago. Henly is single."

"Girlfriend?"

"Kim says no girlfriend. Not for over a year or so. But take a look at this." Rory followed Stroop into the living room where he lifted a large framed photo from a side table. "There must be ten or fifteen pictures of her around. So many that I asked Kim who she was. You know, an ex-girlfriend, a cousin or what? Kim said he'd never met her but that Henly was 'weird' about her. Referred to her as the 'future Mrs. Henly.'" He handed the photo to Rory. "Can't say I blame the guy for dreaming."

Rory studied the image. It was one of those professional vacation photos, complete with date and location in the bottom corner. Three figures huddled together on a long stretch of white sand fronting a perfectly azure ocean. Henly stood on the left. Another tall, dark-headed man to the right and in between, a beautiful brunette in her mid-twenties.

Rory drew the picture closer, blinking hard several times, making sure his eyes weren't playing tricks.

They weren't.

She was slightly younger, slightly thinner, had slightly shorter hair, but those hypnotic brown eyes and that killer smile could belong to only one woman.

Rory's heart sank. His pulse stopped. His jaw tightened so hard his teeth made a wretched grinding sound as he repressed the urge to let a curse slip from his mouth.

*Oh, Tabitha…*

# TEN

"*Thanks for dinner,*" *Tabitha said.*

"*I hope it's the first of many.*"

*The sneer on his face chilled her. She pulled the wool wrap tightly around her shoulders and walked with quick steps to Max's front porch. "Well, I guess this is 'good night.'"*

*He leaned against her and pressed his lips to her neck. "I don't see why it has to be 'good night.'"*

*Tabitha shivered. "Max isn't home yet." She pushed him away. "You should go."*

"*Not yet, baby. Not yet." He shoved her hard against the door, pinning her arms down so she couldn't move…*

"It's just a dream, me girl. Just a dream… Nothing more."

Tabitha awoke to Sasha's sweet whispers. She forced her eyes open, fighting the lingering drowsiness. The dark bunk over her head startled her. She sat up with a jerk, narrowly avoiding a bump to the head, and looked around the strange room. Slowly, she exhaled, remembering that she was at Sasha's brother's home.

Sasha knelt beside her nephew's bed and found Tabitha's hand. "You okay?"

Tabitha nodded and tried to steady her rapid breathing. A cold dampness had spread over her lower back and across her neck. Sweat and Chills, her old friends. Her body twisted through a final tremor.

"You haven't..." Her friend hesitated.

"Had that dream in a while." She shook her head. "No. I haven't. I guess what happened earlier triggered it."

"Undoubtedly. How about some tea?"

"Sounds good."

The two women tiptoed toward the kitchen. Sasha's brother, his wife and their son had a small but cozy home. The kitchen was Tabitha's favorite room, with its bright yellows and blues. She sat at the square maple table positioned in the center as Sasha filled a kettle with water and placed it on the range top.

Tabitha forced a smile at her caring friend. Sasha had been the one hit in the head and tied to a toilet earlier, not her. She should be comforting Sasha, not the other way around. Really, Tabitha didn't know how she would have gotten through the past two years without Sasha's help.

"Was it the same?" Sasha asked, putting two mugs and a box of chamomile tea on the table.

"It started the same." Tabitha wrapped her arms around her body.

"You want to go through it or should I?" her friend proposed.

"I don't need to repeat it tonight."

Sasha looked back at her. "Are you sure?"

Tabitha nodded. "Yeah, with all that's going on right now, it seems almost trivial."

Sasha shuffled to the table and poured hot water into their mugs. "Well, at least tell me what was different."

"I got away."

Sasha's face lit up with a wide grin. "See? You are healing."

Tabitha shrugged. "Well, I got away, but then those two men from the mountain were there." She shivered, remembering their menacing faces.

"Oh, honey. I'm glad I didn't see who tied me up or I'm sure I'd picture them everywhere." She reached over and squeezed Tabitha's hand. Tabitha squeezed back but frowned. "There's more, isn't there?" Sasha asked a moment later.

Shaking her head quickly, Tabitha smirked. "No. You woke me."

"So, you want to go back to sleep and see what happens?"

"Ha. Ha. No, thanks."

"Well, I have to say you seem much better than usual."

Tabitha looked down at the maple wood table, circling a knot with her finger. "I may seem that way, but inside, I'm a mess."

"Want to tell me why?" Sasha slid Tabitha's mug into her hand.

Tabitha nodded, tears already filling her eyes. "Rory asked me out."

"Rory?" Sasha's brows knitted together like she was confused.

Tabitha wrapped her fingers around the warm mug. "Remember? The NCIS agent?"

"Well, duh." Sasha took a deep drink of tea then sat back in her chair. "I just don't understand why that would upset you. I hope you said yes. It's obvious you like him."

"No. No. Remember what happened last time?" Tabitha waved her hands back and forth like an umpire.

"That was months ago. And that guy was a goof."

Tabitha laughed through her tears. "He was not."

"I know. But I made ya laugh. I think you should go out with Rory."

"He makes me nervous. No. He makes me feel safe, and *that* scares me to death. Anyway, how can we even be talking about this, with all these other problems?"

Sasha grinned and shook her head like a mother disappointed with her toddler. "Tabitha, you're stronger than you give yourself credit for. God's going to show you the way."

Tabitha took a deep breath. "It's not God that I don't trust. It's me."

Shaking his head, Rory returned the snapshot of Henly, Tabitha and the other unidentified man to the table. He didn't know what to think. Could it be a coincidence that Tabitha had strange men after her, ransacking her home, just when someone she obviously knew well had been murdered?

He rolled his eyes. Anything was possible, but that was hard to swallow.

Rory needed to find out everything he could about Dr. R. T. Henly—go through the man's home and search every database that he could access. Someone in Henly's field would have been watched closely. There would be plenty to look at.

He glanced at the other man in the picture. Was he important? He could call Tabitha right then and ask her about the connection. He wanted to talk to her anyway. Stealing that kiss had startled her. Perhaps even upset her. He'd been presumptuous in taking it.

Why were things always so complicated? Maybe he needed to forget his attraction to her and get to work. He hoped her attack and break-in had nothing to do with Henly's murder. But if they did, Tabitha might be in more trouble than he'd imagined.

Rory renewed his search in Henly's office. While he skimmed the first drawer of rolling files, his cell chimed. Detective Marks had sent him a picture—of the guy who'd broken his nose on the mountain. The phone chirped in his hand as he stared at the display. This time, Detective Marks was calling.

"Beautiful picture you sent me," Rory said. "Please tell me you've got this guy locked up."

"Afraid not," Detective Marks said. "That mug shot came up when we ran partial prints from Miss Beaumont's home through IAFIS—the FBI's Integrated Automated Fingerprint Identification System."

"I know what IAFIS is," Rory mumbled. "Who is he?"

"Victor DeWitt, a hired thug for a European mob-run organization known as LaPublica," explained Marks. "He's been to trial twice on murder charges, but got off on technicalities both times with a high-priced defense attorney. He's known to work with a man named O'Conner."

"Is O'Conner a tall, blond man, mid-forties with wide-set eyes?" Rory described the other man from the mountain attack.

"Bingo. I'm assuming it's the two from the Hendersonville attack?"

"Yeah. Any idea who they're working for?" Rory asked.

"No. We're still looking. But, Farrell, these guys are dangerous and I can't keep men on Ms. Beaumont after tonight. I don't have that kind of manpower."

Rory pressed his fingers against his forehead, where a sharp ache drummed against his skull. He'd heard of LaPublica. They'd been known to smuggle Western technology into underdeveloped countries. And Marks was right—they were dangerous. Tabitha's security needed to be tightened. Maybe it was time to cash in on his favor with Hausser.

"Have you talked to the FBI?" Rory asked.

"I'll call them next," Marks said.

"When you do, ask for Pat Hausser and drop my name."

"Will do."

"Have you informed Miss Beaumont?"

"Not at this hour," Marks said. "I've got men on her. I'll talk to her tomorrow."

"Right. Thanks for the update," Rory said, thinking he would also call Tabitha in the morning.

He folded his phone and slid it back into his belt clip, considering carefully what the detective had told him. It didn't make sense that a group like LaPublica would go after a worker's compensation lawyer. But a nanotech specialist, now that might interest them.

Rory forced himself back to his search through Henly's belongings. But his mind felt split between the work and his feelings. He couldn't stop worrying about Tabitha.

In the next file, Rory spotted another old photo of her. He swallowed hard. Just how well had she known this guy?

# ELEVEN

Tabitha's left fist steadied her chin over a cup of black coffee. Her other hand dragged a computer mouse aimlessly over a soft rubber pad. A draft of her client's settlement scrolled up and down the screen. The document, full of the usual legalese, did not hold her attention. She hadn't read one line of it.

"You busy?" Sasha's face appeared through the slight opening of her office door.

The interruption yanked Tabitha from the catatoniclike trance. A quick glance at the clock confirmed she'd been motionless for upward of an hour.

"Come in," she said. "You're already finished with your shift?"

Sasha floated in and plopped herself into the plush leather chair for clients. "Nah. The E.R. was slow. They sent me home."

Tabitha closed the file on her computer. "But you don't have a home to go home to."

"Yeah." Sasha twisted and swung one leg over the arm of the chair.

"I've been thinking about that, too. I'd like to go home myself. But Detective Marks insisted I come here. Said it was the safest place. But it's pointless being here. I'm useless. Can't get my mind on a single thing."

"So when can we go home?"

Tabitha shrugged. "Not today. You'll have to go back to your brother's. I'm to meet Detective Marks here after work. Didn't sound good."

Sasha grimaced. "Did you hear from Max?"

Tabitha shook her head.

"How about agent-marine man?" Sasha winked.

"No." Tabitha felt herself blush. "He had a new case. He won't be thinking about me." She looked at his card on the desktop—the one she'd been cradling in her palm half of the morning.

Sasha followed the direction of Tabitha's gaze. "Call him. It's not illegal, you know."

"I don't think so. It's not proper."

Sasha laughed out loud. "You Southerners and all that 'proper' stuff." She stood, shaking her head. "I'm going for lunch. You want salad, subs or Chinese?"

"I don't care. You choose."

Sasha walked out with a wave.

Tabitha reached for Rory's card and tapped it against the top of her desk. She wondered what news Detective Marks would share with her and why he had to do it in person. That made her nervous. She glanced down at Rory's number. She was disappointed he hadn't called.

Settling back into her chair, she grabbed her phone. With a sigh, she put away Rory's card and dialed her brother's office. Max must have been busy, too, since he hadn't returned any of her calls.

"Wake up, Farrell. Meeting with Stroop in ten." NCIS Special Agent Jim Jameson spoke loudly inside the small cubicle.

Too loudly. "Why are you yelling?" Rory lifted his head from his desk. Felt the stubble on his chin then checked his watch. "Ooo. Guess I dozed off."

"Big-time." Jameson laughed. "I tried to bring this to you an hour ago but you were out cold."

Rory took the file from Jameson and checked his watch again. It was close to noon. Last he remembered, he'd called Tabitha. She'd been on another call and instead of leaving a message, he'd decided to give it ten minutes and try again. He shook his head at Jameson. "Why didn't you wake me up?"

The other agent shrugged. "You looked like you needed some Zs. You're the only one who didn't take a break last night."

"I was also the last one to show up." Rory regretted he didn't have all the information he'd hoped to put together before the team meeting. "Are these all the names and numbers from Henly's Palm Pilot?" Rory held up the folder Jameson just handed to him.

"Yep. I made a list of e-mail addresses from his PC, too. I even hard-copied a few of the most recent messages for you."

"Thanks."

"Hope it helps." Jameson smoothed his silk tie across his belly and backed out of the corner cubicle. "See you in ten."

Ten minutes. Rory looked down at his wrinkled black shirt and khakis. He needed a shower, a shave and a large cup of coffee. Ten minutes didn't give him time for anything. Coffee maybe.

He spread the pages from the file across his desk, checking dates, numbers and names. He knew what he was looking for, but not so sure he wanted to find it.

From his search last night, he'd learned the identity of the other man in the beach photo. He was Tabitha's older brother, Max—the same Max mentioned by the men on the mountain and the same Max whose name had been written on the mirror. Max had been friends with Henly for years.

Rory had made another disturbing conclusion. Henly had been more than just a little "weird" about Tabitha. The mad scientist had pictures of her all over his home and even more stored away in albums. The word *obsession* definitely came to mind.

Rory held his breath as he scanned over the pages Jameson had given him. He hated to assume that Henly and Max Beaumont had involved Tabitha in some kind of noxious plot. But where else could this lead? He swallowed hard.

The only thing worse would be if she'd participated in it willingly. But for that to be true he'd have to have seriously misjudged her and he didn't think he had. Tabitha struck him as a woman of faith and morals. Finding old pictures of her in Henly's home wasn't enough for him to change his opinion of her. He didn't know what to think of her brother.

In the documents that Jameson had provided, Rory found what he was looking for—Max Beaumont's address, phone number, work number and cell. Max and Henly had made recent calls to one another and sent several e-mails.

The most recent message, dated last Thursday, was short and to the point.

See you at Stone Grill.

Rory grabbed the entire pile of papers and headed to the meeting.

"Hi, Elise. It's Tabitha Beaumont. Is Max between patients? I was hoping to speak with him."

"Tabitha, I'm surprised to hear from you," said the efficient receptionist.

Tabitha easily pictured the petite, elderly woman seated at the front window of the dental office. Her pencil in hand and the old-fashioned scheduling book spread across her desk.

"Dr. Max took the week off," Elise reported. "I'm surprised you didn't know."

*Surprised?* Tabitha was stunned. Confused. Rubbing her lips nervously with an index finger, she slowly processed the unexpected information, a flicker of hurt and anger rising in her.

First, Max hadn't told her about his weekend getaway and now this? Her brother sometimes did insane, spontaneous things, but they had never included leaving work.

Had the police called him? Did he even know about the break-in or the threat on the mirror? Had those crazy men given up on her and gone straight for her brother? She had no idea. But all of the possibilities seemed grim.

Not wanting to upset Elise, Tabitha kept her shaky voice under control. "I talked to Max on Sunday. He didn't mention it."

"Well, I don't think it was planned. He came in to the office yesterday and worked for about three hours. Then he cleared his schedule for the rest of the week and took off."

"Did he say why, or where he was going?" Tabitha's fingers wrapped tightly around the phone.

"No. I don't ask the boss questions like that. I did overhear him say that he was headed out of town." Elise paused. "Actually, Tabitha, he told us that you'd had a little trouble over the weekend. He seemed really worried. We all thought he'd gone to see you."

*Obviously, he didn't.* But maybe he was coming here, and someone waylaid him? Tabitha swallowed back nausea at the thought of her brother in the hands of the men who had attacked her. "Is Karin with him?"

"I don't know, honey. But she wasn't with him when he left."

"Hmm." Tabitha sighed. If Elise didn't know where Max was, no one else in the office would, either. "Okay. If he comes in, tell him his little sister is looking for him."

"Of course," Elise said. "You take care."

Tabitha pressed and released the receiver then immediately dialed Max and Karin's home. The line rang and rang. Finally, a recording machine answered. *You've reached the Beaumont residence….* Tabitha made a face at Karin's cheery voice on the recorder. This time, she punched the receiver for a new dial tone. She tried Max's cell. When it went to voice mail on the third ring, she grunted aloud in frustration. Where was he? After leaving a quick message, she slammed the phone down.

She had one last option. One other way to locate Max. But it involved doing something she'd never done before.

Calling Karin.

Stroop had already positioned himself in front of the team and started a slide presentation when Rory crept his way to the only open seat in the small conference room.

"…the term *nanotechnology* refers to the control of matter smaller than a micrometer. Research in this area is multidisciplined. The navy's interest in nanotechnology is varied, but rooted in the fabrication of new procedures to enhance and economize all sorts of mechanical, electronic, magnetic, optical and even biological devices.

"Dr. Henly's group worked with updating and developing new weaponry. From his notes and our lengthy interview with one of his division scientists, his most important contribution was a highly efficient self-guided bullet."

Rory felt his eyes widen. He'd heard talk of the idea, of course, but believed it still in the concept stage. If such a device already existed, it was mind-blowing. Not to mention that it gave the word *bullet* from Tabitha's mirror a specific meaning.

*That is, if the cases are actually linked,* Rory reminded himself. He still hoped for many reasons that they were not. At the same time, he couldn't ignore all the phone calls and e-mails that had passed between Henly and Tabitha's brother. It wasn't what he'd hoped for, but the more he uncovered about Henly, the more the man was connected to Tabitha.

With his laptop, Stroop continued to send images to the overhead screen. "Each bullet contains its own nanosystem, or ultra minicomputer. It tells the bullet where to go. The bullets can be programmed by computer before loading or they can be set by laser once they've entered the gun's chamber. With the second option, a gunman marks his target with a special laser and when the bullet is fired, it finds the given mark even if the weapon has significantly changed positions. Every shot is deadly.

"And that's not all. The Office of Naval Research is fairly certain that Henly had further developed this device to explode after impact or even by remote, maximizing damage to the target. At the moment, no one can locate his computer files on this project."

The team of agents shook their heads in disbelief.

"So, Henly was a sellout?" Jameson asked. "We're working the murder of a traitor?"

Stroop tilted his head in a noncommittal fashion. "It's possible. So we're approaching the case in two ways. As a murder *and* as a possible arms sale." He paused for a long moment. "Only a handful of people in the world would have the resources to make a purchase such as this. So far we've come up with three. Fasad Qatier, Anderson Fenton and Yoshito Lan. If Henly was selling to one of these men, then something went wrong. Our priority is to find and secure Henly's files, which we are assuming are on his missing flash drive. If we find it, I have a feeling it will lead us to the murderer. The Secretary of Defense has picked this team for this assignment. Let's not let him down."

As his team filed out of the conference room, Rory waited to be alone with Stroop. He had a lot of information to share.

# TWELVE

Tabitha didn't know exactly why she and her sister-in-law had never hit it off. Certainly, the timing of their meeting couldn't have been worse—just after she'd been assaulted. She'd been dealing with a lot emotionally and Karin always being with Max had irked her. She'd never told Max what had happened. Looking back, she knew she could have spoken to Max privately if she'd wanted. But it had been easier not to. Easier to blame Karin for always being around when really it was her own cowardice and shame that kept her from talking.

Pangs of guilt nudged her conscience as she realized she wasn't even sure she had her sister-in law's phone number. She should have made more of an effort to befriend the woman.

Flipping through her old-fashioned Rolodex, she found nothing listed under Karin Gill. But she mostly used the Rolodex to organize business cards. She buzzed her assistant. Jane didn't have the number, either.

*Think, Tabitha.*

During their wedding, she must have scratched Karin's number down in case she'd had a problem with her bridesmaid dress or something. But where? She hoped it wasn't at home in that wreck of a house.

Tabitha tapped her fingers over the desktop. Why was she so worried about her brother anyway? Was it just paranoia that made her think he might be in trouble? Maybe Max and Karin had gone off somewhere together. Another honeymoon. She should just let them be, dealing with her problems alone.

The office line rang and Tabitha jumped. She hated being so edgy. Reaching for the receiver, she realized how badly she hoped her brother held the other end of the line, how badly she wanted him to put an end to this nonsense. "Tabitha Beaumont."

"We're doing Chinese. You want Kung Pao Chicken or Pork Lo Mein?" Sasha's voice blasted through the receiver, competing with the equally loud car stereo.

"Maybe just some soup." Tabitha tried not to sound disappointed.

"You okay?" Sasha asked.

Tabitha sighed. "I still can't get a hold of Max."

The car music turned off. "Other than that, you okay?"

"I'm really worried about him—"

"It won't hurt to call Karin, ya know," Sasha suggested.

"I can't find her number."

"I have it," Sasha said.

"You do?" Tabitha paused. "Why?"

"Well…I'm not really supposed to say."

"Sasha! This is no time for secrets."

"Okay, okay. At the wedding, Karin asked me about places to visit in Ireland. She wants to surprise Max with a trip. We didn't finish talking so she gave me her number. She didn't want you to know…afraid you would let it slip."

Tabitha felt the rub. "Oh."

"Well, do you want the number or what?" Sasha asked.

"Of course."

Tabitha wrote the number down, hung up with Sasha and immediately dialed her sister-in-law.

"Karin?"

"Yes, hello." Karin's alto voice held a hint of Southern aristocrat, a subtle reminder of her upper-class status. In the background, Tabitha heard the sound of wind and surf. She imagined Max and Karin basking in the sun on a warm beach and sipping cold drinks. Her cheeks grew red with fury. She had people chasing her down and ransacking her home while the two of them relaxed on the shore. The impulse to hang up surged through her. "This is Tabitha. I'm sorry to bother you but—"

"I thought that might be you. I saw the North Carolina area code. Max said you just loved your tri-athlete tournament over the weekend."

"It was a race and I didn't finish." Tabitha covered her mouth. Why did Karin bring out the worst in her? The woman was just trying to make conversation and she had responded so rudely.

"Oh…I'm sorry. I'm sure you'll win next time, especially after you and Max work out together this week."

Tabitha blinked a few times. Then her heart sank to her stomach. "Work out together? What do you mean? Max isn't with you?"

"Don't be silly. He's with you," Karin corrected.

Tabitha gasped. The letters *M-A-X* across the mirror drove through her mind. "Karin, I haven't talked to Max since Sunday night and I certainly haven't seen him. I'm at work."

"Tabitha, you tell your brother if he wants to play a joke on me, he should try something funny." She giggled as she spoke.

Tabitha agreed this wasn't funny. Where was her brother? "Karin, where are you?"

Her sister-in-law stopped giggling. "At my father's home on the shore. I came down yesterday. Max said I should visit my dad since he would be with you through Friday."

"With me?" Tabitha touched her hand to her temple where she could feel her pulse pounding. "He's not with me. But I need to tell him something. We need to—"

"Tabitha, come on. Quit kidding around. I hate jokes."

"I'm not joking. Karin, how long would it take for you to get back to Richmond?"

"About four hours. Why?"

"I need you to—"

"Tabitha, really," Karin interrupted. "Stop teasing and let me talk to Max."

Tabitha sighed. Her sister-in-law didn't grasp the seriousness of this situation. But why would she? From the sound of it, she knew nothing of what had happened over the weekend. Tabitha decided to enlighten her.

Five minutes later, a very solemn Karin was on the other end of the line. The words between them were brief and emotional. They decided to meet in Richmond and hunt for Max together.

"We'll find him," Tabitha declared. She ended the call and buzzed her assistant. "Jane, I have to go out. Send my calls to voice mail. If anyone needs immediate help, send them to one of the paralegals."

"No problem. Anything else?" her assistant asked.

Tabitha hesitated, hating to consider the risks she was taking by leaving her office without telling Detective Marks. *I have to find Max. Please, Lord. Let this be the right thing to do.*

"Yes. I've had an urgent family matter come up that needs my immediate attention. I'll be out a few days. Reschedule my court dates."

As she clicked off with her assistant and shut down her computer, she glanced again at Rory's card. Should she tell him her plans? Her hand hesitated over the phone. She let out a shaky breath. No. It'd be better to wait. She'd go to Richmond and talk to Karin first. Then she'd call him. Maybe.

Tabitha retrieved her purse from her desk drawer and headed out. As she pulled open the door, Sasha bounced in with a big take-out bag. A heavenly smell permeated the small office.

Sasha took one look at Tabitha with purse in hand. "What's wrong?"

"Max is missing," she announced. "I need to meet Karin."

"I thought ya weren't supposed to leave?"

Tabitha pulled the key to her rental car from her bag. "Well, this is an emergency."

"Tabitha, shouldn't you call the police?"

"I can't."

"Why not?"

Tabitha made a big gesture with her hand. "Remember the wedding? If the media got wind of it—"

"I know. They love Karin's family and all the money. I was at the wedding. Okay then." Sasha put down the bag of food. "I'll come with you."

Tabitha shook her head. "Not this time, Sasha. You're better off at your brother's."

"Well, at least take an egg roll."

Tabitha grabbed one, gave her friend a hug and hurried off.

Rory had been sitting for so long his legs had started to go numb. He jiggled them up and down to get the blood moving. The NCIS-issued sedan didn't have the amount of legroom his truck did. His truck, unfortunately, did not make a good stakeout vehicle.

Rory rubbed his forehead and checked his watch. The chances of Max Beaumont showing up at his own house seemed slim to none. The man wouldn't answer his phones and hadn't been to work since yesterday morning. His wife, too, had gone missing.

Rory grabbed his cell phone and dialed Tabitha's office for the third time. He'd almost memorized the number. The voice mail picked up again, so he clicked off. He'd already left a message. He was considering calling Marks when his phone chirped.

Stroop. "Still no action?" his boss asked.

"No, sir. Nothing at the house. And as you know, his office told me that he went to visit his sister. She's supposedly at her law office but I haven't gotten through. Any news on your end?"

"A witness. At the Stone Grill. You know, the pub in Georgetown mentioned in Henly and Beaumont's e-mails," Stroop reminded.

Rory pressed the phone closer to his ear. "So, they were there?"

"Yes. The dentist and the victim met there Friday for lunch just like they'd planned. A waitress identified them both. She also said they came back. Yesterday."

"Yesterday?" Rory sat up straight, bumping his head on the roof.

"The waitress said Beaumont showed up around two thirty for a late lunch. She remembered because he sat down right when she was about to close her station. Said if he hadn't been so cute she would have told him she was closed. Then she said that 'the big guy,' meaning Henly, came in around three. The two of them had words. Didn't eat their lunches. And by three thirty, both had left. But not together."

"Anything else?" Rory asked.

"Not on Beaumont. But Jameson found Henly's offshore account. Ten million and some change. He opened it three months ago."

"I'm guessing that's a lot for a nanotech engineer."

"That's a lot for anybody. Farrell, why don't you get back to headquarters? I don't think you're going to find Max Beaumont in Richmond."

"No, sir. Probably not." He threw his phone on the console and started the engine.

Rory glanced down the street at the majestic brick Georgian with its wide front portico and massive columns, the home belonging to Max and Karin Beaumont. The mail sitting in their box suggested no one had been there for two days. Nothing was happening here.

Rory waited five more minutes then turned his agency car around to head out of the posh neighborhood. At the first stop sign, a white Acura passed him. His eyes followed it in the rearview mirror as it pulled into Beaumont's drive. Glad he'd waited that five minutes, Rory circled the block and went back to his observation spot.

# THIRTEEN

The loud chimes of Max and Karin's doorbell sounded within ten minutes of Tabitha's arrival. Karin's little puppy yelped then scrambled toward the noise. Tabitha and Karin followed.

"Who is it?" Karin asked through the closed door.

"NCIS Special Agent Farrell."

What? Tabitha's heart flopped into her stomach. She scooted Hoover aside and plastered her eye to the peephole. But even seeing Rory, she could only half believe he was there. She turned to Karin. "I know him."

Karin sidled up to the peephole. "I thought we agreed no police."

"I didn't invite him."

Karin grunted.

The doorbell sounded again and Hoover let out another yelp.

"I'm conducting an investigation," Rory said, his voice muffled by the closed door. "Open up, please."

Tabitha reached for the knob but Karin pulled her hand away. "I'll get it."

Karin picked up her puppy, cradled him in her arms like a baby, then cracked the door just enough to look out, but not far enough to expose Tabitha.

"Mrs. Max Beaumont?" Rory asked.

Karin nodded.

"I'm looking for your husband." Rory held out his agency ID.

"Well, I can't help you. I don't know where he is," Karin said stiffly and began to shut the door again.

"No, Karin." Tabitha stopped the door from closing.

As Karin shifted her weight, Hoover leaped down and went for the door. He took one look at Rory and changed his mind. Turning on his hind end, the puppy clambered to the back of the house. Karin trailed after him.

Tabitha turned to Rory. His eyes were steely, like they'd been when he'd grilled her on the mountain. Cop mode. Her hands shook as she pulled the door wide. "Are you really looking for Max? Or are you following me?" Her mouth was so dry she could barely get the words out.

"I'd like to come in," Rory stated, his expression flat.

Tabitha stood aside, allowing him to enter. She closed the door and they stood facing each other in the foyer. No one spoke. Tabitha could hear her own breath going in and out.

"Well," she said at last. "I guess you need to speak with Karin?"

Rory did nothing but nod once.

"This way." She indicated.

In the kitchen, they found her sister-in-law sitting on a tall stool behind the breakfast bar, holding a tissue in one hand and a cup of coffee in the other. Her head hung low, almost touching the counter. Hoover was happily occupied in his kennel, chomping away on a large rubber toy.

"Karin, this is the agent I told you about. The one who helped me. Rory, this is my sister-in-law, Karin Gill-Beaumont."

Karin dismissed the formal introduction with a wave of her hand, not even looking in their direction. She didn't offer him a drink or a seat. Tabitha blushed, embarrassed by Karin's rude behavior. She indicated an empty stool for him to take.

"No. Thanks. I'm tired of sitting." He pointed to the carafe of coffee whose freshly brewed aroma filled the kitchen. "But I wouldn't mind a cup of that."

"Fix the officer a cup, would you, Tabitha?" Again, Karin didn't bother to lift her head.

Tabitha turned toward the coffee. She couldn't stop her eyes from rolling in response to that air of superiority Karin sported. Until this afternoon, she thought that was all there was to Karin. But today she'd seen a different side of her sister-in-law. The poor woman had been frantic, thinking Max was having an affair. Even after Tabitha told her what had happened on the mountain and explained about the break-in at her home, Karin seemed unconvinced. She couldn't understand why Max would have lied about his whereabouts. Tabitha was not so certain that he had.

"That's not his title, Karin," Tabitha corrected.

"No. It's okay," Rory said. He walked to the edge of the bar where Karin sat and leaned against the countertop. "She's right. I'm an officer. Mrs. Beaumont, I need to speak with your husband as soon as possible. It's urgent. Do you have any way to contact him?"

Karin lifted her head. A scowl covered her expression as her eyes grazed over his figure. "If I did, do you think I would look like this?"

Tabitha poured Rory a steaming cup of coffee and elaborated on Karin's answer. "Max left yesterday for work and Karin hasn't seen him since. He told her he was on his way to visit me. He's contacted her by phone once, but now he's not answering his cell." She lifted the mug. "Cream? Sugar?"

"I like it black. Thank you." He took the cup from her hands, avoiding any contact with her fingers.

"Can you tell us why you need to question Max?" Tabitha asked. "Is it about what happened over the weekend?"

Rory's eyes fixed on his mug. "I'd rather speak to Dr. Beaumont first. Do you expect him to call again?"

"Maybe tomorrow. But who knows?" A nervous laugh escaped Karin's mouth.

"Mrs. Beaumont, I'm sorry," he continued. "I know this is upsetting. But I have some questions for you, as well. Why don't you take a few minutes alone? Collect your thoughts. That way I can speak with Tabitha first."

Urgency showed in Rory's tight expression. Tabitha felt her own level of tension increase.

"Don't let me stop you." Karin didn't bother to hide the irritation in her voice.

"I need to speak with your sister-in-law in private," Rory clarified.

Karin glared at them. But then she stood and left the room.

"Why did you do that?" Tabitha scolded him in a whispered tone. "Can't you see how upset she is? She believes Max is cheating on her. And now she thinks you want to talk behind her back." She moved past him. "I'll see if she's okay."

"Let her go." His hand came tightly around her elbow.

Tabitha shot her eyes up at him and tried to pull out of his grasp. He released her but stood in the space between the two cabinets, trapping her inside the kitchen. The look on his face showed he had no intention of letting her escape. Tabitha swallowed hard and forced herself to match his hard gaze, somewhat surprised and pleased to realize that even with him boxing her in, she didn't feel trapped or afraid.

"At least now I know why I kept getting your voice mail." Rory's voice was low and strained and dotted with sarcasm.

"You called me?" She looked away. *And I wasn't there.* Pangs of guilt knotted her stomach.

"More than once. I was about to call Detective Marks and see what he'd done with you. Tabitha, I know he would never have okayed this road trip."

Tabitha's eyes skirted around the room. "I was going to call Detective Marks. But Karin was so upset. I had to get here as soon as possible. We're worried that—"

"How about you talk to Detective Marks right now?" He handed his cell phone to her. It was already ringing. She supposed directly to Detective Marks at the Charlotte PD.

Tabitha drew in a deep breath. It seemed Rory had been keeping close tabs on her. She couldn't bring herself to resent it. She should have called him about Max. Leaving Charlotte on her own had not been wise.

When Marks answered the line, Tabitha explained what she'd done. The detective seemed satisfied. He asked to speak to Agent Farrell. She passed Rory the phone. As he listened to the detective, his eyes stayed glued to her—still on the cold side, but maybe a little less angry than before. At length, he clicked off and took a long drink of coffee. "I see your ankle is better."

"Yes, it is. Thanks. Any news about my house?"

"Yes. The Charlotte PD identified one of the men who broke into your home."

Her pulse quickened. "Really?"

"A man by the name of Victor DeWitt." Rory took another drink then continued. "I saw his photo. It's one of the men who attacked you on the mountain."

"Which one?"

"The shorter, bald one with the bad scar across his cheek."

A cold chill traveled up Tabitha's spine. "What does this mean? Is there a connection between him and Max? Is that why you're here?"

Rory lifted a brow. "I don't know the answer to those questions."

"Well, what do you know?" Tabitha hated to sound so irritated, but Rory was stalling or fishing for something. She could feel it.

"I know he was the same man that grabbed you on the mountain, the one that broke my nose. And I know that he's a hired gun for LaPublica."

Tabitha felt her mouth fall open. "LaPublica? Is that some sort of political group?"

"No, but they started out that way." He paused. "Now, it's a European mob organization."

"Well, I don't practice law for them, if that's what you're insinuating." Tabitha crossed her arms over her chest.

Rory's brow furrowed. "Are you getting defensive again?"

"Are you interrogating me again? I thought you came to question Max."

"I did."

Another awkward silence passed. They both drank from their coffee mugs and stared at each other. Tabitha's irritation stewed. Why wasn't he telling her what he knew? He was the one who had the information. He was the one who'd shown up unannounced at her brother's home. "So, will the police be able to catch this DeWitt person?"

"Men like DeWitt are not easy to find." Rory shifted his weight and put his mug on the counter. "Tabitha, you should have stayed in your office today, like Marks told you to."

He sounded more worried now than angry, his eyes reflecting concern. "I should have," she agreed in soft tones. "I'm sorry if I worried you or caused problems. But my brother is missing. If I didn't know that he'd canceled patients and packed a bag, I'd believe this DeWitt person already had him. And even with that knowledge, I'm still not sure. What if DeWitt grabbed him, the way he tried to do with me, on the mountain?"

"I told you if you had a problem to call me."

"I know. I know." Tabitha felt her eyes getting moist. "Please don't be upset with me. I didn't know what to do. I wanted to find Max. I didn't want to bother you." *I was afraid.* Tabitha turned away, head down, and busied herself by rubbing a hand towel over the clean countertop. She refused to cry in front of Rory Farrell again.

"What did you think you and Karin could do?"

Tabitha shrugged. "Call Max's friends and check the computer to see if he used an ATM or a credit card. You know, like at a hotel or something."

Tabitha could sense Rory stepping toward her. She could feel his gaze on the top of her head, hear his soft exhale, smell the deep musk of his cologne.

"You should have told someone what you were doing," he whispered. "You took a great risk."

Turning to his voice, Tabitha found Rory stood closer than she'd thought. She flinched in response. "I'm sorry. I didn't mean to cause problems."

Tabitha could feel her nerves swirling inside her as if caught in a whirlpool. She knew Rory hadn't driven all the way to Richmond to tell her that he was worried. There was something else. "I know you're not here to give me a lecture. Can you tell me why you need Max? Didn't he talk to the police like he was supposed to?"

Rory let out a long sigh. "Your brother did talk to the detectives in Hendersonville. First thing Monday morning. I'm not sure about Detective Marks. If your brother talked to him, Marks didn't mention it."

Rory brushed her hair off her shoulder then traced a finger over her jawline. A pleasant chill joined her stressed nerves.

"So, is that it? Is that why you're here?" Tabitha swallowed hard, knowing that wasn't it. Why would a federal cop come to question a man about his failure to check in with the Charlotte PD? He wouldn't. Rory had come as an NCIS officer. He'd said so when he'd first arrived. Apparently, she couldn't think straight with his hand on her cheek. She was glad he backed away to the other side of the kitchen.

"Tabitha. I'm on a case that involves questioning your brother. I don't know if it has anything to do with what happened to you."

She rolled her eyes. "And that's all you can tell me?"

Rory squeezed his forehead with two fingers. "Okay. Maybe you can help. What can you tell me about Dr. R. T. Henly? I believe he was friends with you and your brother."

Tabitha's eyelids flickered. "Who? What? You

mean…Roger? Roger Henly?" The words stuck in her throat. She didn't know if she was blushing or if all color had drained from her face. Either way Rory had to know that he'd struck a nerve. A big one.

She scrambled to regain her composure, willing her breathing to steady. For two years, she'd done it every time Max, Karin or her parents talked about Roger. She would do it with Rory, too. She focused on her answer.

"Dr. Henly. Sure, I've known him for years. He does research for the Navy. Are you investigating him?" Now *that* she could believe. "My family has known Roger since he was in high school. He and my brother were good friends, especially close when Max went through his party stage. I don't think they do much together anymore. He didn't come to Max's wedding." A blessing for which she'd be eternally grateful.

"What about you?"

A lump rose in her throat. Her voice faltered. "Wh—what about me?"

Rory hesitated and she wondered what he already knew. Her heart pounded against her chest.

"What was *your* relationship with Henly?" he clarified.

"Oh." She drew in a deep breath. "I haven't seen Roger in years. He was Max's friend… Why all the questions about Roger?"

"He's dead."

"Excuse me?" Tabitha took a step back and grabbed hold of the countertop.

"Dr. Henly is dead. Murdered actually. I'm investigating his death."

Tabitha slumped over the counter, trying to process Rory's statement. "When?" The question barely sounded from her lips.

"I can't really share the details—"

"Last night," she interrupted. "When you got that call and left so quickly." She didn't wait for him to confirm her assumption but closed her eyes and reminded herself to breathe.

*Roger dead.* The strangest feeling of emptiness spread

through her. At one point, she'd really cared for Roger, seen a goodness, a kindness in him. But after he'd gotten drunk and hurt her, she'd hated and feared him. Now, his name or any thoughts of him left her cold. Angry. Shamed.

"Tabitha. Are you okay?" he asked. "I thought maybe you'd already heard. It was on the news."

"I hadn't." She turned and forced her body to move across the kitchen. She needed a moment alone.

"Excuse me," she said as she passed by Rory.

Rory reached out to steady Tabitha as she tried to leave the kitchen. Her face had turned so pale. He doubted her ability to walk to the next room without stumbling. With one arm behind her shoulder, he led her to a long couch in an adjoining sitting area. She resisted his help for the entire twenty feet. He was used to it. The fear and darkness in her eyes he also recognized. But her expression held something new. Since the very moment he'd mentioned Dr. Henly, she'd looked almost numb. She wasn't speaking casually about a friend of the family. Her expression had become too flat, too detached. He didn't know how to interpret it, but it disturbed him.

"I didn't mean to upset you," he apologized, regretting the way he'd told her about Henly's death so abruptly. It had been a heartless ploy to get a reaction.

"No. Really. I'm okay," she insisted. "It's just been a long day." Her voice sounded weak, as if she struggled to get the words out and in the right order.

"Tabitha?" Again, he tried to make contact with her hand, just a light touch to calm her. She pulled away.

"Stop. I'm fine."

Rory worked hard to remain calm but he couldn't stand her reaction to him. It had been a long time since he'd felt such tenderness in his heart for a woman, and to have her flinch away when he only wanted to help cut him deeply. "Why do you do that? Why do you pull away from me like that?"

A nervous sigh escaped her lips. "I don't like being helped. Remember?"

"I don't think that's it. And it's not because you despise contact with me. A minute ago, I did this…" He reached slowly across the sofa and touched a gentle finger across her cheek. She stiffened and fought the urge to recoil. This time he saw the fear in her eyes. "This isn't about Henly…" Or was it? Rory swallowed hard. His mind reeling as he put the pieces together. "It is about Henly, isn't it? Did he stalk you? I know he was obsessed with you. Your pictures were all over his condo, in albums, everywhere. Tell me what he did."

But she didn't need to. Rory could now read the whole horrible truth in her eyes.

Tabitha whimpered and continued to draw away to the other side of the couch. "Roger didn't stalk me. I knew him. That's all. I wasn't prepared for that news. It's tragic."

"And I say you look scared, not sad. I think it's time for you to tell me that long story we skipped over the other day."

# FOURTEEN

A few tears had rolled down Tabitha's soft cheeks. Rory wanted to wipe them away. He ached to hold her, but he didn't think he could handle watching her flinch away from him again. "Tabitha, talk to me."

She sniffed hard and wiped her eyes. "Okay. Sure. It's no big deal. If you have to know, I went on a date with him. It was about two years ago. It didn't work out. I'm sure it's not important to your case. Now, if you'll let me, I'd like to rest for a minute." She rose from the couch and wobbled. "You need to talk to Karin. I'll find her."

Tabitha's body shook so hard that Rory didn't know how she managed to speak or walk. He hoped she could make it across the room. Terror and pain filled her expression. Any hurt and disappointment he'd felt over her leaving Charlotte unannounced had disappeared and been replaced by a desperate longing to comfort her. Because he knew now that Henly hadn't stalked her; the man had raped her.

"Please, Tabitha, talk to me." Rory stood.

Her body quivered. "There's nothing to talk about. I'm sorry… I just have a sudden headache. Talk to Karin. She's probably in her office down the hall."

Tabitha had obviously practiced her ability to control her emotions. Maybe that was why he'd never detected this before. Why she'd been so amazingly calm after the attack on the mountain. That experience had been mild in comparison. Even now, she'd composed herself enough to walk out of the room without faltering. He started to follow, but she lifted a hand to indicate he should stay put. She didn't want him. And he wanted to be with her now more than anything. He wished to hold her and share that hurt which had broken her heart. It didn't matter what her brother was or what he had mixed her up in. He didn't care. He yearned for this woman to open up to him and trust him.

And he knew it was too much to ask. Tabitha might be a long way from ever trusting a man. If she ever would...

Rory sat on the couch again and lowered his head to his knees, running his hands back and forth over his short hair in frustrated strokes.

*God, could You be with her? Take her fear and her pain.* His doubting faith stopped the flow of words. Did he dare believe in the power of a prayer? The loss of his father, the anger he held inside had crippled his trust. But today he pressed his uncertainties aside.

*I know You're there. I know You're listening. We both know that I'm still angry. I admit I don't understand Your ways and I don't know if I ever will. I don't know why You would help Tabitha when You didn't help my dad. But I'm asking You to...*

*I'm asking. And I guess that's something....*

Tabitha had taken the back stairs. He could hear her light footfalls traveling overhead. He might as well do as she'd suggested and talk to Karin.

Rory found Tabitha's sister-in-law in the downstairs study and knocked at the opened door.

"Come in, please," Karin said calmly.

Mrs. Beaumont had cleaned her face and changed her clothing. She wore a simple black top, white pants and pearls, and had applied some light makeup around her red eyes. Her appearance pronounced elegance and sophistication rather than emphasizing her features.

"I apologize for my rudeness earlier," she continued. "I was mad and hurt. I thought Max was having an affair. But you wouldn't be here if it were that simple. I realize that now."

"I know you must be worried, Mrs. Beaumont."

"Call me Karin. Please."

"I hope you don't mind answering a few questions."

"If you think it will help find my husband, I'd be happy to."

After ten minutes, Rory could hardly believe that Karin and Tabitha knew the same Max Beaumont. Karin described Max as serious, hardworking and predictable—a nearly complete contradiction to the free spirit that Tabitha loved so dearly. There were common denominators, however: Max loved God and his family.

"That's why I married him," Karin explained. "I knew right away that he didn't want my money. He wouldn't even take any from my father at our wedding. Max has depth and character that I've seen in few people. I love him and he loves me. If Max is in trouble, I want to help."

"What about his relationship with his sister?"

"They're very close." Karin turned back to her computer screen. Apparently, she didn't have much to say about Tabitha.

Rory scanned the titles and snapshots on the built-in bookshelves. "Tabitha said that you were looking for ATM and credit-card charges."

"Yes. It's a little sneaky. But after Tabitha told me what happened to her. What those men said…"

"Have you found anything?" he asked.

"One withdrawal in town. Yesterday, just before noon. But nothing since. I even checked our investment accounts."

"Mrs. Beaumont—"

"Karin." She shook her head in protest.

"Karin, I assume you know most of your husband's friends?"

"Of course. All of them." She smiled, a well-practiced debutant pose.

"How about a man by the name of Henly?"

Her smile faded fast as she turned away from the computer monitor. "Max visited with him last weekend. Roger was out of the country during our wedding. So he and Max had lunch and then Roger gave Max our wedding gift. It's a painting he'd had. I'd fussed over it once and I guess he remembered."

"How nice." Rory thought about the missing art in Henly's condo. "So, when was this? I understood Dr. Beaumont was away most of the weekend."

"He saw Roger on Friday. Then he and I drove to Annapolis for a weekend sailing trip."

Rory nodded. "You didn't want to go with him to pick up your painting? Seems like Henly's place in Reston would have been on the way to Annapolis."

"I was invited, of course, but I had an appointment." She paused. "And, to be completely frank, Roger's not my favorite of Max's friends. I don't know how Tabitha could stand him. They used to date, you know."

A shooting pain struck Rory in the neck. This family had secrets. Karin would not have said something so callous if she'd known the truth. He gave her more credit than that. Made him wonder if Max knew.

Rory's guess was no. Or, at least, it seemed unlikely that Max knew on Friday. Surely, he would not have picked up a wedding gift from the man. That didn't seem in character from either Tabitha's or Karin's description. But what if Max had found out since Friday about Henly attacking Tabitha?

Rory rolled his head back to relieve the dull ache. The throbbing only increased. He felt desperate to check on Tabitha. "You said the painting is here? I'd love to see it."

Karin seemed pleased. "We hung it in the den." She stood from behind the desk and moved into the next room. "It's a Fredrik Vasloh. Roger has several of them. I'm surprised he parted with it. It's a very generous gift."

Exactly what he'd been thinking. Too generous. Rory took a quick look, pretending to admire its lines and colors. It was definitely the same style as the others that had graced Henly's fancy home. What could Henly have meant by giving it to Max? Was it really a wedding gift? Or a payment? Maybe a bribe? Perhaps even an apology for his horrid behavior with Tabitha? Rory wanted to be sick right there in Karin's den.

Rory sighed and backed away from the artwork. "How long did Dr. Henly date your sister-in-law?"

"Oh. I don't know. It was before I met Max. Apparently, Max and Roger spent a lot of time together before…" Karin paused to study his figure as if seeing him as a human for the first time. He didn't like it. Perhaps Karin had realized that his last question had been personal.

Rory fidgeted with his tie and stepped toward the hallway. Karin had given him plenty of information to work with. He needed to see Tabitha. Now.

"Agent Farrell," Karin said, stopping him at the door. "Why so many questions about Roger? Do you think Max could be with him?"

Rory met her green eyes. "No. I don't." The disappointment in her face caused him to swallow hard. "Would you mind if I checked on Tabitha? She went upstairs with a headache."

"Perhaps I should go," she suggested.

"Actually, I'd like to talk to her again."

Karin frowned but pointed to a set of stairs near the kitchen. "The guest room is at the top. She'd be in there."

"Go away," Tabitha responded to the soft knocking at the bedroom door.

"I'm coming in." Rory's voice warned her gently. The door opened slowly.

Tabitha turned her face away from him so he couldn't see that she'd been crying. "I have nothing to say to you about your murder victim."

"I'm not here about that. I'm here about you." He entered the generously sized room and approached the side of the bed where she sat hugging her knees to her chest. "Will you talk to me? Friend to friend. No cop stuff."

"I don't want to talk. I especially don't want to talk to you."

"You need to talk about this."

"Not to you I don't."

"I care about you." Rory put a hand on her shoulder. Tabitha didn't try to stop herself from flinching. She was thankful he had sense enough to remove it.

Still, she felt his gaze caress her. When she looked up, his eyes held genuine warmth and concern, which made her sad.

Tabitha liked Rory. She truly did. She liked the way he moved and the way he went after what he wanted. She liked the way he looked at her and smiled. She liked the way her stomach flip-flopped when he was near. She even liked his gentle touch despite her body's occasional unwelcoming reaction to it. She wished they had met under different circumstances.

"Maybe you do care," she said. "But I don't think you know how to separate cop stuff from friend stuff. And if you're working Henly's murder, then you're looking for a motive. I'm not stupid, Rory. I'm not telling you anything that could hurt my brother."

Rory stood motionless for a moment. Then he removed his coat and loosened his tie. He took a small wooden chair from the corner of the room and placed it at the edge of the bed, making a seat for himself near her, but not too near. She turned her head to face the other side of the room.

"Can I tell you about one of the first cases I ever worked for NCIS?" he asked.

*No.* "Sure. Whatever."

"It was five years ago. I was a probationary agent stationed in Norfolk, right out of training. A woman named Sara, a first lieutenant stationed at Oceana, called and said she'd witnessed a crime.

"I was so green. I was actually excited to question her. So, I hustled over to her apartment with my partner. But when we arrived she wasn't there."

Tabitha lifted a hand. "I already know I don't want to hear the rest of this story. There's a reason I'm not a criminal lawyer." She shook her head. "Please don't tell me you found her dead."

His eyes cut at her then darted away again. His lips pressed together, like he wasn't too sure he should continue. "I found Sara at Portsmouth General. She had a mild concussion and two broken ribs."

Tabitha closed her eyes. She didn't like this ending, either. Her head dropped between her bent knees, hiding her face.

Rory moved beside her on the edge of the bed and pressed a shoulder against her tucked-up legs. "Someone Sara worked with had sexually assaulted her. That was the crime she wanted to report. She wasn't a witness. She was the victim."

A sea of emotions flooded through Tabitha. She didn't know if she'd ever felt so vulnerable and exposed since her ordeal with Roger. She'd gone to such lengths to hide the truth, even from the people she loved and trusted. Now this man, practically a stranger, comes along and sees right through her. Well, she didn't want his pity any more than she wanted anyone else's.

She lifted her head and looked him in the eye, compressing her own mixture of emotions into the one she could use to her advantage. Anger. Its bitterness fell from her lips. "This is ridiculous. We're wasting time. We should be looking for Max."

Rory's expression didn't change. And when she stood from the bed, he didn't reach for her as she'd anticipated. Instead, he blocked the door. "Move, Rory."

He ignored her request. "Sara was so afraid. I'd never seen anything like it. No matter what I said to her, she wouldn't talk to me. I've never seen fear like that in anyone. Not even in the Middle East when my team knew that snipers had surrounded us. This fear was different. Mixed with shame and self-blame. It was deep. I've never forgotten her. Or that fear I saw in her."

Tabitha bowed her head, determined not to cry, not to show him how much his words affected her, hurt her, angered her. "Stop. Stop talking. Sara's story is tragic but it has nothing to do with me or why we're here."

"It may have nothing to do with the case. But, Tabitha…"

She looked up with a scowl. Fury loosened inside her. Why was she doing this? Her emotions were fragile enough without him cracking them open and spilling them out for the whole world to see. Why couldn't he let it go? Why couldn't he get out of her way?

Rory reached out to her. "Tabitha, you said yourself God sent me to help you… Well, here I am. I want to help. You need this. You're angry and hurt. Talk to me." He took a small step toward her.

"Stop." Her hands balled into fists. Her jaw tightened. She wanted to scream. Rory was too close. The walls were too close. The room seemed to be growing smaller and smaller. Tabitha couldn't breathe.

"I see that fear in you," he continued. "Not all of the time. You're good at hiding it. But sometimes it's there and you need to let go of it. You need to—"

"Enough," she hissed. Her whole body began to shake uncontrollably. Her fists pressed hard against her temples, where the throbbing made her brain feel as if it would split in two. Rory closed in the final step between them and Tabitha struck out at him. "How dare you! How dare you say you know what I need!"

He stopped her first punch, but the second, the third, the fourth hit him in the chest. An unstoppable wave of emotion, all the anger and hurt she'd pent up for two years, unleashed. "How could you? How could you?" *How could you, Roger?*

She still hated him. Hated what he'd done. She hadn't forgiven him. Or herself.

Finally, her body collapsed. Rory opened his arms to her and she fell exhausted and sobbing into his embrace.

"I thought I forgave him. I said the words. I prayed it so many times. And I really meant it, but I'm still so angry. So hurt. I think I still hate him."

"Shh," he whispered. "You need to be angry. It's part of healing. If it makes you feel any better, I hate him, too. If he weren't already dead, I might have done the job myself."

Tabitha knew by his tone, he'd meant it as a joke. It was well-timed and helped her calm herself a bit. She pulled back just enough to wipe the wetness from her cheeks. "When you told me that he died, part of me thought 'Good. He can't hurt me anymore.' That's terrible, isn't it?"

He kissed the top of her head and drew her back to his chest. "No. You hate what he did to you. You think he took your pride and strength. But he didn't. If anything, you're stronger. And you're right to find relief in his death. Now he can't hurt another woman, or hurt you again. And that *is* good. Your pain will lessen in time. You'll forgive him when you're ready."

Shame flowed through Tabitha and she turned away from Rory. He was wrong. Roger still hurt her, still pained her, still made her feel broken. Not good enough to be loved. "I don't know. I don't know if I'll ever be who I was before."

Rory circled Tabitha to cup his hands gently around her face, drawing her eyes to his. "Every experience changes us. I think we have to accept that."

Tabitha winced. "And it's that easy for you? Like your father dying? Is that so easy to accept?"

"No. I didn't say it was easy. I have my own battles which I would love to share with you another time. But let me tell you what I see in you. I think you are the most beautiful, most amazing woman I've ever met in my life and if I had just half of the faith and strength that you have in your ear…your little ear right here…" He touched his finger to her left ear. "I would be… I'd be… Well, we're not talking about me, but it would be an improvement. Let's just say that. You make me feel like a better man just being in the same room with you."

His words fell over her, strong and heartfelt. God had sent Rory to her, but he was hard to accept. He charged at her like a bull one minute and then held her like a teddy bear the next. He confused her with all the things he made her feel. She wanted to thank him for letting her rage out but she had no words.

He pulled her back into his arms. "I'm going to kiss you right now. Stop me if you want."

As he leaned down, she looked into his big blues—dark oceans she found herself swimming in. That kiss she wouldn't have stopped for anything. It was kind and soft. Without words it told her she was beautiful and cherished...and safe.

# GET 2 BOOKS

**IF YOU ENJOY A ROMANTIC SUSPENSE STORY** that reflects solid, traditional values, then you'll like *Love Inspired® Suspense* novels. These are contemporary tales of intrigue and romance featuring Christian characters facing challenges to their faith…and their lives!

We'd like to send you two *Love Inspired Suspense* novels absolutely free. Accepting them puts you under no obligation to purchase any more books.

## HOW TO GET YOUR
## 2 FREE BOOKS AND TWO FREE GIFTS

1. Return the reply card today, and we'll send you two *Love Inspired Suspense* novels, absolutely free! We'll even pay the postage!
2. Accepting free books places you under no obligation to buy anything, ever. The two books have combined cover prices of $11.00 in the U.S. and $13.00 in Canada, but they're yours to keep, free!
3. We hope that after receiving your free books you'll want to remain a subscriber, but the choice is yours–to continue or cancel, any time at all!

## EXTRA BONUS

**You'll also get two free mystery gifts! (worth about $10)**

# FREE!

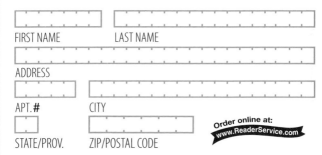

# FIFTEEN

Tabitha wanted to stay in Rory's arms a little longer. She couldn't seem to pull away from the way it made her feel, so beautiful and whole.

He, too, seemed reluctant to back away, but he did. "Not that I want to move. I don't. But…" *There's work to be done,* he left unsaid.

"You still haven't explained why it's so important for you to find my brother."

The kind expression that had pronounced the crow's-feet at the corners of Rory's eyes disappeared. His lips pressed together. He grabbed his coat from the edge of the bed and walked to the door. Tabitha didn't like the grim air that had settled around him.

"Let's go downstairs. I'll talk to you and your sister-in-law at the same time." He sighed and held out a hand for her.

*Friend-hot. Cop-cold. Hot-cold. Back to cold.* Her heart and brain could hardly keep up with his transformations.

They found Karin in the study at her desk, staring at the computer screen. Rory led Tabitha into the room and over to the sitting area. Then he walked back to the door.

"I'll be right back." He disappeared before anyone could ask what he was doing.

"Is your headache gone?" Karin asked.

Tabitha turned to her. "I didn't really have a headache."

Her sister-in-law looked miffed. "Well, if you were discussing Max's whereabouts I want to hear. I want to know what's going on." Desperation laced her words.

"Roger's been murdered."

Karin gasped. The seriousness of her husband's situation settled in quickly. Her face went rigid.

"Rory's looking for Max has something to do with Roger's murder," Tabitha added.

"But what could Max know about that?"

"He didn't say." Tabitha took a seat in one of the large wingback chairs. "Has Max even seen Roger lately? He didn't come to your wedding."

"Last weekend. He and I went to Annapolis together on Saturday. But on Friday, Max must have seen Roger because he came back with the Vasloh."

Tabitha shook her head. "You didn't like Roger much, did you?"

"No. I didn't." Karin looked up and her tough expression softened. "Oh, dear. I'm sorry, Tabitha. I know you were close with him a few years back. You must be upset about his death. You've been crying. I can see that now."

"Come sit over here, Karin." Tabitha pointed to the neighboring armchair. "You might as well know the truth."

"The truth about what?" Karin settled into the chair next to Tabitha.

"Two years ago, Roger and I went out together. Not for long. A few dates." Tabitha worked hard to steady her voice.

"Yes. Max said that you broke up with him. Is that not what happened?" Karin leaned toward her, green eyes wide.

Tabitha hesitated. "Max doesn't know about this."

"About what? Tabitha, what happened?"

There was only one way to say it. "Roger violated me. I was staying with Max that night. We all went out. Roger and I got to the house before Max. Roger had had too much to drink. He forced his way into the house and… Well, he forced me."

Karin reached for her hand.

"I should have reported him. But— He was Max's friend for so long. Once he sobered up, he cried and begged me not to. Told me he'd do anything for me. I just wanted him to leave. I just wanted him out of my sight. Forever."

Karin relaxed into the large chair. "So, you told everyone that you didn't have enough in common with him and you've avoided him ever since."

Tabitha nodded.

"Oh, Tabitha. How could Max and I not have seen this? You have to tell him."

"Well, let's just find him first."

"We should pray," Karin suggested.

Tabitha couldn't hide the surprised look on her face.

Karin grinned. "I met your brother at a Bible study. It was my first time. He's taught me so much."

"I didn't know." Tabitha realized that she hadn't learned much about her sister-in-law.

Karin squeezed her hand and now Tabitha wanted to cry for a completely new reason. She had sorely misjudged her brother's wife. It humbled her. All this time she'd tried to forgive Roger when she was the one who needed forgiveness.

Karin led a sweet and heartfelt prayer, asking that Tabitha find a love like the one she had with Max and for Max's safe return to them. When they looked up, Rory stood in the doorway. Tabitha motioned for him to come in. "I told Karin what we talked about upstairs."

"Good. So, she knows why I'm here." Rory entered, carrying a large metal suitcase. After placing it on an ottoman, he looked over at them and forced a smile.

"We assume it's because you knew that Max was with Roger on Friday," Karin theorized.

"And again yesterday afternoon," he said, explaining about Roger and Max's meeting in Georgetown.

Karin's brows knitted together. "Then, why aren't you looking for Max in D.C.?"

"My team isn't ruling that out. There's a bulletin out for his vehicle. We're checking area hotels. I need to know if you ladies will help me. My boss wants to collect Max's fingerprints. Is there anything that only he would have touched?"

Karin protested, but Tabitha assured her it was better to let Rory do his job without interference. "Max could be in danger. We need to do what we can to find him."

Karin relented. "Try the master bathroom. All his toiletries are there. He has a spare set for travel. Would you like for me to show you?"

"No. Thanks. I'll find it." He started upstairs with the case.

"I don't like this," Karin whispered as he left the room. "Did Agent Farrell tell you anything else about the murder or his case?"

Tabitha shook her head. "Not really. I'm hoping he'll explain when he comes back."

From the Beaumonts' bathroom, Rory sent the prints he'd collected over his scanner and called Stroop. All forensic evidence collected from Henly's condo had been logged in the NCIS system, so Beaumont's prints, if they had been at the crime scene, would show a match.

"Matches found in Henly's kitchen and living room," Stroop reported. "None in the study where he was killed."

The fingerprints still placed Max in the condo, reinforcing the doubts he had about Tabitha's brother. Max had a lot of circumstantial evidence linking him to Henly's death. *And a possible motive.*

For a moment, he considered telling his boss about Tabitha's past. But he feared doing so would end his relationship with her. She might never trust him again and he wasn't willing to risk that. For now, he would assume that Max didn't know about what had happened between Henly and his sister. If circumstances changed, he could ask her to make a formal statement. But that decision he'd leave to her.

"Henly's missing painting is here. Mrs. Beaumont claims it's a wedding gift," he said, putting away his materials.

Stroop coughed. "Agent Jameson said those paintings are worth about a half million each. That's a nice wedding gift."

"I thought so, too. Did Jameson find anything about DeWitt or LaPublica?"

"We came up with a company called BonTech or BT. It operates a nanotech facility in France. Interpol suspects them of involvement with LaPublica."

Rory lifted his case and headed out of the bathroom. "Suspects what, exactly?"

"BT makes hardware and software. Jameson is working on a financial link. But I think we already have one. Guess who have been BT employees for the past three years?"

Rory stopped at the top of the staircase. "DeWitt?"

"And O'Conner," Stroop said.

"How about Henly's ten mill?"

"Jameson traced it to Kuala Lumpur and from KL back to Switzerland, *La Banque Nationale*. The bank that, of course, handles—"

"BT's finances." Rory finished his boss's sentence.

"More specifically, their payroll."

"So, Henly sold his nanobullet technology to someone in LaPublica who will use BT to produce the bullets. DeWitt is the collector. But probably not the lead on the purchase," Rory concluded. "Any other news?"

"Yes." Stroop's tone seemed to lighten. "From the Charlotte FBI Field Office."

"Oh, yeah. Hausser sent a couple of men to Tabitha Beaumont's house after the break-in."

"Well, he called just minutes ago and said he's taking the Beaumont case from the Charlotte PD. He wants to know if you can handle Ms. Beaumont until he sends for her. I agreed to this, but I couldn't inform him of her connection to our Henly case… Since he heard she was with you, I can send someone down," Stroop continued. "A guard for Miss Beaumont and her sister-in-law."

"No." Rory paused, trying to separate his feelings from the case. It was impossible. "I'd like to keep an eye on Ms. Beaumont while I look for her brother. Maybe he'll contact her."

"Don't let this get personal, Farrell. She's connected somehow. That can't be good."

Rory disagreed. As far as he was concerned, everything about Tabitha was good. He didn't like the idea of putting her in someone else's care.

"But you have a point," Stroop conceded. "If she and her brother are as tight as you say, and DeWitt is after her, she may expedite the search. Maybe she knows something she hasn't thought of yet. I'll give you twenty-four hours in Richmond. Let's hope she can lead us to Henly's files."

Rory shifted his weight. "And Max's wife? She doesn't seem to be part of this."

"Send her somewhere with protection," Stroop answered. "There's an FBI safe house in Richmond if you need it."

Rory clicked off with Stroop and headed to the study with his large case. He had no intention of letting Tabitha out of his sight, but his motives for keeping her around had nothing to do with finding Max or Henly's files. He wanted to protect her and didn't trust anyone else for the job.

In fact, finding her brother had taken on a whole new focus. Possibly Max could help the case, but more important it would make Tabitha happy and that had suddenly become very important to him.

While Karin answered more questions for Rory, Tabitha made sandwiches and poured tall glasses of iced tea for the three of them. She hoped it would help restore some physical and emotional strength. She had a feeling that to find her brother, she would need it.

Rory had surprised her when he'd returned from upstairs. Evidently, along with the assignment of finding Max, her safety had been placed in his hands. And yet he'd insisted that Karin be escorted by personal guard to her father's secure estate in Charlottesville. Mr. Gill had already sent his personal driver— a man also trained in the martial arts—to fetch her. Although Tabitha wanted to trust Rory, separating the two of them seemed strange. He had never said whether he believed Henly's death and her attack were connected, but she suspected it herself. Why else would he keep her around? Why not send her with Karin? Either he cared about her that much or he needed her for his case. The way she had felt a few minutes ago in his arms, she didn't know if she wanted to learn which was the truth.

One thing was certain—the search for Max was not entirely based on his recent lunch with Roger. There had to be other factors. Like Dewitt mentioning Max's name and writing it on the mirror in her home. She wondered what Rory thought of the fancy Vasloh painting. The timing of the excessive wedding gift seemed a bit suspicious, even to her.

She'd never remembered Roger being so generous. In fact, he'd been terribly proud of that art collection. He'd even installed a special security system after he'd bought it, boasting it protected his "retirement plan."

How naive she'd been to think that Roger had any goodness in him! The man was selfish to the core. He'd lied to her about so many things…everything that mattered, really. There was only one thing he'd been honest about—admitting he'd do whatever it took to become a rich man.

Tabitha shook her head. *Whatever you did, Roger, it got you killed.* She hoped he hadn't enticed her brother to join in.

Tabitha's heart palpitated unsteadily as she walked to the study. The porcelain plates and tea glasses on her tray clinked and clanked until she crossed the room and placed it on the coffee table. Hoover, the puppy, playfully licked the air as he picked up the scent of food.

"Did you find anything?" she asked Karin and Rory.

"No." Rory smiled kindly at her. "Karin was just telling me about your brother's lack of interest in computers." His eyes turned hungrily to the sandwiches. "Those look good."

"Turkey and cheddar," Tabitha said proudly. "Help yourself. Karin, you should eat. I'm going to, as well."

She handed everyone a drink, a sandwich on a plate and a napkin. Rory thanked her with soft eyes. She wondered how he switched their look from hot to cold so smoothly. Somehow, the phenomena annoyed her and attracted her all at the same time.

"I've been thinking we should search Max's work," Tabitha suggested.

"You're right," Karin agreed. "Unfortunately, it's after hours. The office is locked up. I don't have a key. But Paul does."

Tabitha turned to Rory while Karin arranged for Paul to meet them.

"This is delicious," he mumbled, devouring all but the last bite, which he fed to Hoover. "Unusually spicy."

"Hoagie sauce," she replied. "You know, I'm glad you talked Karin into going to her father's. She'll be able to get some rest there. But I'm surprised you want me to stay. Won't I just slow you down?"

Rory licked a spot of sauce stuck to his thumb. "DeWitt came after you. Not your sister-in-law. If I had known who he was when we were in Hendersonville, I'd have never let you go home without protection. And don't worry. You won't slow me down. I think you can help."

Ah. The real reason. Her help. Like she could help. Did he think she would not understand? Rory didn't care about protecting her. He just cared about his job. *Find Max Beaumont. Use whomever and get a motive while you're at it.*

As much as she wanted to believe that Rory felt something for her, she was afraid to totally trust him. Max could be a suspect in Rory's murder case. Why not? She'd come up with the idea herself.

"I don't know how I can help," Tabitha said flatly.

"Paul will be there in thirty minutes," Karin interrupted. "And I see my ride is here." She pointed out a nearby window to her bodyguard and driver standing under the front portico next to her father's limo. She went upstairs and returned after a few minutes with a small overnight bag. Hoover loped after her on a short leash. Rory and Tabitha followed her into the foyer, where she handed Tabitha a key. "This is to our house, if you need a place to stay or rest."

Tabitha smiled and put her arms around Karin for the first real hug she'd ever exchanged with her sister-in-law. "I misjudged you."

"I gave you little reason to like me," Karin attested. "I was never too sure how to respond to your family—not being close to my own the way you are with Max. But I'm learning. Find Max, Tabitha. I don't care what he's done." She pulled away.

Tabitha swallowed hard. Did Karin still suspect Max of being involved in an affair? Or did she think he was mixed up in Roger's murder?

"Max hasn't done anything. He's not like that. You and I both know it. This is all a mistake." She spoke loudly, hoping Rory heard.

Karin and Hoover rode off in the limo with the personal bodyguard and, two minutes later, she and Rory locked the house and headed to the dental office in his car.

Tabitha sat back, arms crossed over her chest. Her suspicions about why Rory had kept her around had transformed from curiosity into anger. "Now would be a good time to tell me exactly why you're looking for Max and why you need my help. Do you hope I'll lure him out of hiding?"

"What!" he gasped. "I don't need you to lure him. Where did you get a crazy idea like that?"

"It's not crazy. It's the only explanation for keeping me along."

"That's ridiculous." His eyes cut at her. "You have no idea how I feel about you, do you?"

Tabitha fell silent.

"I care about you," he continued. "I don't trust anyone else to keep you safe. It's that simple. I need your brother because he was seen with Henly within two hours of the murder. He's probably the last person to see him alive."

"You mean, besides the killer," she reminded him.

"Right. Besides the killer."

Tabitha turned her head toward him in disbelief. Her stomach churned. "You think my brother killed Henly!"

"I don't know who killed Henly. I just go where the evidence leads." He stretched out his hand but she quickly removed hers from his reach.

"I don't believe you," Tabitha said. "You say you care about me. But you just want to do your job. And right now that's finding Max and pinning him for murder." She could have kicked herself for being so weak in front of him, for exposing so much of herself. She should have known better. Tabitha buried the tenderness she had begun to feel toward him. No more. She could not afford to make another bad decision about a man.

Rory directed the agency car into the parking lot of her brother's office in silence. He stationed the sedan in the middle facing the front of the building. The Beaumont and Michaels Family Dentistry sign was across the front doors.

Tabitha wiped her moist eyes and looked for Paul's car, but her brother's partner had not arrived.

"Tabitha," Rory began softly, cutting the engine. "There is no direct evidence linking your brother to Henly's murder. And there's no motive. I'm not sharing what you told me with anyone. And I never will. That's a promise. That's your story to tell, not mine. But I'm glad you shared it with me. I know you don't want to trust me right now and I can't blame you. After all you've been through, I understand that. But it doesn't change the fact that you can trust me. I am looking for your brother. I need to find him. For the case, sure. But mostly I want to find him for you."

Tabitha sat up and looked at him. The gold from the low setting sun reflected in his eyes, giving them added gentleness. She wanted so badly to trust him. She just couldn't.

"What about the painting from Roger to my brother? Do you think it's really a wedding gift?" she asked him.

"I don't know. All that's certain at this point is that your brother was with Henly close to the time of the murder, that a hired gun mentioned his name and is after you, his sister. It's not good that he's missing. Look, Tabitha. This is personal for me. I have feelings for you and that makes a difference. If you want me off this case, I'll call my boss right now and bow out. He'll send someone else to look for your brother, and you and I can go sit somewhere safe until this is all over."

His voice, his words, his expressions, softened her heart. She wanted to find Max and she wanted to trust Rory. But could she do both? Was she willing to try? "I'm not going to sit and do nothing while my brother is in trouble."

"But do you want *me* to look for him or someone else?"

"You," she whispered. She couldn't face this alone. And if trusting Rory turned out to be the wrong decision, then God help her. God help her, anyway.

"When we find Max," Rory stated, "he can tell us what's happened. He can set this straight. Until then, let's just concentrate on finding him."

She nodded reluctantly. When he let the tough cop persona drop, Rory talked so sweet and looked at her as if he cared more about her than anything in the world. Lifting her hand to his lips, he kissed the back of her fingers. She closed her eyes and relaxed her hand in his. *God give me strength. I'm so afraid.*

"Trust me," he said.

If he only knew how hard she was trying. Tabitha opened

her eyes, focusing on the locked office in front of them. "You know what I keep thinking?"

Rory lifted his brows. "What's that?"

"That the longer my brother is missing, the greater chance he'll end up like Roger."

# SIXTEEN

Rory watched Tabitha exchange a quick handshake with her brother's partner.

"Thanks for meeting us, Paul." She turned to Rory. "This is Special Agent Rory Farrell."

"I know," Paul said stiffly. "We met this afternoon."

Tabitha glanced from the dentist to him. "I came here first," Rory explained, putting a hand gently on her shoulder. Maybe she wanted to trust him, but he could see that she struggled terribly with the idea—ready for it to fail at every turn. He couldn't wait to prove her wrong. He turned back to Paul. "Nice to see you again, Dr. Michaels. We appreciate your cooperation."

"I can't believe Max is missing," Paul said. "Of course, I'll help in any way I can."

The dentist unlocked the first set of double glass doors, pushed inside and disarmed the initial alarm. Tabitha followed him, while Rory watched from behind, wondering just how much Michaels would really help them. He'd been less than informative when they'd met earlier that afternoon. Dressed in full scrubs, Michaels had enjoyed playing the man in charge. Rory suspected he only got to do that in Max's absence.

Tonight, Dr. Michaels appeared less sure of himself. Donned in some high-end tennis attire, he waddled to the inside doors and security panel. Rory watched as his sausagelike fingers punched in the four-digit code.

"Kids are always trying to get their hands on our nitrous oxide," Paul said. "We had to install this elaborate system to put an end to the break-ins." He unlocked the other set of double glass doors, using a different key.

"I didn't know you played tennis," Tabitha remarked casually.

"Just started." His round face feigned a smile. Rory noticed, too, that for a dentist, he didn't have very white teeth.

"I'm sorry we interrupted your match," she added.

"Oh, it hasn't started yet. You know, Tabitha, I noticed your new crown is ready. While I'm here, I could replace that temporary."

Tabitha cut her eyes at him like brown daggers. "I'm not really worried about that right now."

Paul raised his palms in the air and backed away. "Okay. Sure. Just thought I'd offer. Well…I guess I'll get back to the tennis club… That is, if you don't need me."

Rory rubbed a hand over his mouth to conceal his irritated expression. He'd noted Paul's indifferent attitude earlier, but this beat all. His partner is missing and he's worried about a tennis match? Then again, without Paul there, they could search the place unhindered. He moved aside as Paul passed through the entryway.

"Do as you like. You don't need to stay," Rory said. "But I'll need a number where I can reach you in case I have questions. And we'll need keys to any locked cabinets. And computer passwords."

Paul started to hand over the ring of keys then pulled them back to his chest. "I thought you guys were just looking through Beaumont's office. Don't you need a warrant to search the entire place?"

Tabitha looked as if she might strangle the little guy.

"It's all the same, Dr. Michaels. As long as you agree to the search, we're okay," Rory answered calmly. "Mrs. Beaumont has done so on behalf of her husband."

Paul looked from Rory to Tabitha then down at the keys, finally handing them to her. "Well, of course. I was just curious.

Anything to find my partner. My number's on the key ring if you need me." He moved away.

"Computer passwords?" Rory reminded him.

"Oh, right." Paul gave a half laugh on the way to his Jeep Commander. "There aren't any."

"Should we set the alarm when we leave? What about the keys? Don't you need them back?" Tabitha called after him.

Paul barely slowed down to answer. "Leave the keys at your brother's. I have another set. The alarm is easy, two-seven-two-one. You have thirty seconds to get out."

That said, he shut his car door, started the engine and peeled out of the parking lot.

Tabitha turned back with widened eyes. "I guess he was running late. I've never seen him so…" She searched for a word. "I was going to say *weird*, but now that I think about it, he's always a little weird."

"I don't like him."

"I could tell." She smirked.

Rory lifted an eyebrow at her then put his hand comfortably at her back, leading her through the double-door entry and across the dark waiting room. The sun had fallen low and with no windows in the front office, the space felt like a closet, dark and closed in.

At the receptionist's area, Tabitha hit a panel of lights, illuminating the front end of the office.

"Max's jersey numbers from high school," she whispered.

"What's that?"

"The code. Twenty-seven, twenty-one. They were his jersey numbers. JV and Varsity."

"We'll find him," Rory promised, running a hand through her long, soft curls. When she didn't cower, he wanted to cry out for joy. Then she smiled at him for the first time that day.

"I really like it when you smile." He paused and moistened his suddenly dry lips, but took a step back, forcing himself to remember why they'd come. "Okay. You start in the operatories. I'll check your brother's office." He headed down the hallway.

"What am I looking for?"

Rory turned back. "Anything connected to your brother or Henly. Correspondence. Computer storage."

"Computer storage?" She made a strange face.

"Yeah, computer storage." He started to tell her about Henly's missing data then decided against it. "And lock those doors."

In the back office, Rory booted up the computer on Max's desk. When it came to retrieving history from a hard drive, Rory was not the efficient operator that his partner, Jameson, was. But he surprised himself, reviewing Max's computer activity from Monday morning in minutes.

At 7:50 a.m., Dr. Beaumont had checked his schedule: 8:00 a.m. crown delivery, 9:30 a.m. filling, 2:00 p.m. root canal.

At 8:48 a.m., Beaumont logged back in and read e-mails. None seemed to be of any interest. Around 9:15 a.m., he'd searched the Web, looking at sailboats on eBay.

Rory began searching through the desk. Light footsteps approached the office. Tabitha stopped at the doorway and leaned against the dark wood frame. Her big brown eyes stole his breath.

"Find anything?" he managed to ask.

"No. Just the usual stuff. I don't see anything that could help us. Unless you need painkillers or dental explorers."

"Hmm. No, thanks."

Tabitha tilted her head, resting it against the door frame. "Should I look through patient files? I think they're behind the receptionist's area."

"Yes. Start with your own, your brother's and Henly's. I'll keep poking around in here. Maybe call another agent to help me retrieve more from the computer."

She nodded. "Okay. I was thinking of calling Karin myself to make sure she made it to her father's."

"I think she'd appreciate that."

Tabitha turned on her heels and walked out. Rory listened to her fleeting steps as she moved down the long hall to the reception area. The woman made his heart dance. The feelings he experienced when he thought of her, when she was near, he'd never had in his life. Not for anyone. He shook his head and dialed the agency.

"What's up, Farrell?" The harsh voice of Agent Jameson drew Rory's lovesick mind back to the case.

"Need computer help," he said.

"What's new?" Jameson teased then coached Rory through some operations that searched the files on Max's computer.

Waiting for the results, Rory noticed the light to the phone's second line illuminated. Tabitha must have placed her call to Karin.

Several minutes passed and Jameson's tests had recovered little, and nothing of any value.

"Well, it was worth a try," Rory said. "Got any other news?"

"Uh…yeah. Hey, hang on, Farrell. Here's an update coming in." Jameson paused briefly.

Rory checked the light on the second line. Still green. The call to Karin seemed long. He hoped everything was okay.

"They've located Beaumont's car," Jameson reported. "At a gas station near Georgetown."

"And Beaumont?"

"No. No dentist, just his car. It was parked, locked and empty. No trace of Max Beaumont."

"Karin, did you make it home?" Tabitha balanced the receiver between her ear and shoulder then plopped the patient files onto the desktop to review.

"We're not far now," Karin said. "Ten minutes or so. How's the search? I see you're still at the office. Find anything?"

"I'm checking files. Rory's checking Max's computer."

"I doubt he'll find much on there," Karin said with a chuckle.

"I know. But it's worth a try."

"Yes, I hope he finds something. He seemed genuine about trying to help."

"I guess," Tabitha replied. "I'm not sure his motivation is the same as yours or mine."

"He seemed pretty concerned about you. I'm glad he's looking for Max."

Tabitha put her face between her hands and rubbed her forehead. Why did that thought, which seemed to comfort Karin, turn her insides out? "I just hope we find him soon. Let us know if he calls you."

"Sure."

Tabitha said goodbye and reached to hang up the phone as the lights over the reception area and waiting room went out. She stood quickly and reached to the switch plate. The sudden transition into total darkness overwhelmed her senses. Disoriented, she grabbed the edge of the desk to steady herself.

Behind her, she heard the heavy exhale of someone close. A squeal formed in her throat as cold metal pressed hard into her temple.

"Don't make a sound or I'll blow your brains out, and when your GI Joe bodyguard comes running down the hallway for you, I'll blow his out, too." The voice was male, gruff and slightly familiar.

Tabitha swallowed away the scream. In the darkness, she could see nothing but the lights on the telephone. The dull dial tone pulsed from the open receiver she'd dropped to the floor.

"Sit." The man shoved her into the receptionist's chair. "Put your hands behind you and clasp them together."

He pivoted the chair so that she faced the wall. As she spun, Tabitha noticed the panel of buttons overhead.

The dentists' call buttons.

The receptionist used them to signal Paul's or Max's offices, to let them know when a patient was ready and waiting in the chair. Tabitha knew if she could reach the right button, Rory would hear a quick buzz in the back office—one that would not sound in the reception area. Maybe it would make him suspicious. Or, at least, curious.

But the panel was a good two feet above her and the man had already bound her hands together behind her back. She shifted her weight in the chair as she eyed the buttons. How could she reach them?

"Don't even think about knocking your chair over," he warned. "I've still got the gun on you."

Tabitha didn't question him. From what she could tell, he used only one hand and his mouth to pull the string around her wrists. The cord felt tight and cut into her tender skin.

"You're not getting away this time," he mumbled.

That voice. She knew its evil from the mountain. The image of the bald man returned to her like a ricochet—his hollow gray eyes, that hideous scar on his left cheek, his tight grip on her wrists. Victor DeWitt had found her.

Tabitha's limbs became dead weight. She couldn't breathe. A black wave of panic flowed through her—so intense her body started to shut down. She slumped into the chair, as darkness rode over her.

The barrel of the gun ramming into her neck shocked her back to consciousness. A high-pitched whimper came from her lips.

"Shut up, you stupid broad," DeWitt muttered.

"Where's my brother?" Tabitha whispered. She had to focus on Max. Forget her fear.

DeWitt pulled her by the hair, lifting her from the seat. He yanked her head back against his neck and chest. The contact made Tabitha's stomach revolt. He kept the gun under her jaw and spoke low. His lips pressed against her ear. "Don't worry. He's next."

*He doesn't have Max! Thank You, Lord.* She wanted to squeal again, but this time from relief. Max could still be alive. With a surge of hope, Tabitha focused on the call buttons just inches from her shoulder. It was her best chance. Maybe her only chance. She had to hit them and signal Rory.

DeWitt urged her toward the waiting room. Tabitha purposely caught her foot on the wheel of the office chair and threw her weight toward the wall. DeWitt took a handful of her hair, but he didn't fire. Her shoulder and forehead hit the wall before he yanked her back to his chest. She prayed she'd hit a few of the buttons, hopefully the one connected to Max's office.

DeWitt cursed under his breath and shoved her into the waiting room and toward the front doors. Tabitha did as he urged. Through the doors, she saw a large black SUV at the curb—no doubt the same one from the pizzeria parking lot.

DeWitt pressed her toward the doors and the SUV. She needed to stall him. But how? He had a gun at her throat. Tabitha held her breath and prayed for her life as DeWitt pushed her through the first set of doors.

# SEVENTEEN

The phone call to Karin was taking too long. A feeling of uneasiness crept over Rory, making the hairs on the back of his neck prickle.

After ending his call with Jameson, he shut down Max's computer and began searching through a few of the desk drawers. He pulled out an address book and thumbed through the pages.

Again, he checked the light on the phone. Still green, but it no longer gave him reassurance. Tabitha didn't strike him as the type to chat on the phone in any situation, but especially not with her brother missing. Either Karin had some important news for them or Tabitha was no longer on the—

A loud buzzing sound broke the silence in the office. Rory bolted from the chair, his senses thrown into high alert. A small button under the switch plate began to flash a red light. It was some sort of call system for the dentists, something Tabitha wouldn't have used unless she was in trouble.

Adrenaline filled Rory's veins as he leaped to the door and killed the lights. He drew his Glock and peered down the long corridor. Darkness blocked his view. The lights Tabitha had turned on in the reception area were out.

*Please don't let me be too late. Please.*

Rory glanced back at the red signal light on the wall, but from which room had the signal been sent? Tabitha could have hit the call button from any number of rooms. He'd start with the reception area since that's where she had headed.

He ran low to the ground with his gun out, straight to the front desk. The small space was empty. The receiver hung to the floor. A dull busy signal hummed. He cursed the sound of it. How long had the phone been off the hook?

Rory looked for the file room when he caught the lights on the call panel. Three buttons blinked. If Tabitha had activated them from that very spot, she couldn't be far.

A faint swoosh sounded through the receptionist's window and then a draft of air pulled through the space. The front doors were opening.

Rory turned the corner into the small waiting area and took aim. "Stop or I'll shoot."

The man who held Tabitha by the hair flipped her around and slid behind her in one quick move. Slowly, he dragged the barrel of his pistol from her neck to her temple, scraping it hard against her skin.

Rory had no shot. The man and Tabitha had passed through the first set of doors and with Tabitha as a shield, Rory couldn't risk it.

"I forgot to lock up," she cried. Her hands had been tied behind her back. She looked horrified and in pain.

"Shut up, broad," the man holding her yelled.

Under the soft emergency light of the entry, Rory recognized the bald head of Victor DeWitt. His finger itched to pull the trigger.

"And you." He looked at Rory. "Drop your weapon."

DeWitt yanked Tabitha back against himself and pressed the gun hard on her temple. Rory winced as Tabitha whimpered in pain. He lifted his hands and turned his Glock so that he held it by one finger. Keeping his eyes fixed on Tabitha, he lowered the gun slowly to the ground.

DeWitt started pushing his way through the second set of glass doors, pulling Tabitha along with him. Rory saw the vehicle waiting for them by the curb.

"Leave the lady. She doesn't have the files. Her brother does and I know where he is." Rory spoke in the calmest voice he could manage. Negotiating. He had to negotiate. He wished he'd paid more attention to those lessons at the academy.

DeWitt ignored the declaration and continued to slide between the doors. He seemed concerned about his distance to the car. Rory understood. He would have to expose his backside to enter the vehicle and he knew Rory might overtake him.

With DeWitt's eyes on the vehicle, Rory made a move toward the doors. Two steps closer.

"Forget it, cowboy." DeWitt's gun came down and aimed at him.

Rory froze, lifting both hands in the air. At least DeWitt's gun pointed at him and no longer at Tabitha's head. Tabitha must have had the same thought because she suddenly threw her body into DeWitt as hard as she could, slamming into his outstretched arm. DeWitt went out through the doors. His gun fired twice, but Tabitha had forced his aim wide. The bullets broke the panels of the inside doors. Chunks of glass shattered. Rory shielded his face from the flying shards.

Head lowered, he grabbed his gun and moved toward the doors. Tabitha had dropped or fallen to the ground. She lay facedown in the entryway. He crossed over her and stepped out of the building just as DeWitt jumped into the car. The vehicle peeled away.

Rory had no angle on the SUV that didn't involve the busy highway in front of Max's office. He couldn't shoot. He had to let him go. Again. He took note of the license number and ran back to Tabitha.

"Don't move. You're covered in glass." He grabbed his phone and dialed Emergency. Then he bent over Tabitha's body and began to pick the pieces of glass from her back, arms and hands.

"I must have forgotten to lock the doors. I'm sorry." Her body shook with emotion.

"Shh. Don't talk and try not to move."

Tabitha trembled and jerked as he worked over her. Twice he cut his own fingers on the sharp glass. The flakes caught on his face itched terribly. But their removal could wait. Tabitha's wounds looked deep and painful.

"I'm not so sure you didn't lock the doors," he assured her. "They don't look too hard to pick. DeWitt is a professional. Those two-key dead bolts might keep kids out, but they're not going to stop someone like DeWitt. Anyway, you were great. You hit that call button and knocked DeWitt outside. You even pushed his arm wide so I wouldn't get shot. I appreciate that. If you weren't covered in glass, I'd hug you."

A muffled giggle shook her body.

"Stop moving," he scolded.

"Stop making me laugh."

"You know, what you did was instinctive and gutsy. I've met some law enforcement agents who don't have such good impulses. You should consider a career change."

"No, thanks." She winced as he removed a rather large piece from her shoulder.

"Sorry. I'm trying to be gentle."

"I know." Her body relaxed somewhat. "I think I've seen that SUV before."

"Where?"

"In Charlotte. On Sunday. I was waiting for Sasha to pick me up at Joe's Pizzeria. A car like that came into the lot and circled around. It creeped me out. I got nervous and ran back inside."

"And you're just now telling me this because…"

"Because I thought my nerves had gotten the best of me. I'm glad now I went back inside the restaurant."

"Me, too." He sighed, wishing he could tell her just how glad he was.

A fire truck, an ambulance and a squad car arrived quickly. Rory allowed the EMT crew to treat Tabitha while he spoke with the police officers.

Paul Michaels had been notified of the break-in and showed up about twenty minutes after the police arrived, just as Rory finished giving his statement. Rory handed him the keys and left him to talk to the officers. He found Tabitha sitting in the back of the ambulance with a blanket wrapped over her shoulders, sipping orange juice.

"They said I'm good to go." She feigned a smile. "Liquid stitches are great. And they gave me some antibiotic cream." She held up a little plastic tube for him to see. She sounded groggy.

Rory nodded, knowing she had to be exhausted. He needed to get her somewhere she could rest. He'd arranged for them to stay at the FBI safe house that Stroop had mentioned earlier. He hoped she would consent.

Rory led Tabitha to his car and helped her in. She cringed as she tried to sit back against the leather seat.

"Where to?" she asked, as he turned the car around and pulled out of the parking lot.

"I think after that last episode, we should head to the safe house."

She nodded. "Is that where Max is?"

Rory's heart sank. Tabitha had believed his pathetic attempt at negotiation with DeWitt. He shook his head. "No. I don't know where Max is."

"I didn't think so. And what files? Did you find something on Max's computer?"

Rory wiped his mouth with his hand, pausing to think over his answer. A person could only handle so much at a time and Tabitha had had more than her share for the day. Any more information could wait for tomorrow. "I didn't get anything off the computer... You know, Tabitha, right now the only thing I'm concerned about is you. You need some real sleep. The EMTs gave you a painkiller that will knock you out for a while. So we should probably—"

"You mean, you told them to give me a painkiller." She

narrowed her eyes. "I wondered why they didn't even mention a trip to the hospital."

"You can thank me later," he said. "The meds will hit you soon. So, before you're out, let's get to this apartment. Can you help me navigate? We're looking for the corner of Park and Stuart."

"That's close to where my dad teaches. Take a left here. And hurry. My head's getting woozy. And just for the record, I'm really mad at you."

He laughed. "Sweetheart, you've been mad at me most of the day."

The safe house was in a small apartment building in the section of Richmond that Tabitha called the Fan. She explained the name came from the fanlike pattern that the streets formed as they spread westward from the hub of the city. Rory wasn't sure, at this point, if Tabitha knew what she was saying. The painkiller had definitely hit the bloodstream. Her speech was slow and her eyelids drooping. Thankfully, her directions were still accurate, and they reached the apartment building without mishap. He helped Tabitha into the building, taking special care not to make contact with any of her wounds.

A young man dressed in jogging shorts and a T-shirt answered the door to the apartment. "I'm Special Agent Carter. I've secured two rooms for you." He glanced at Tabitha limp in Rory's arms. "Looks like you need one of those now."

"Please."

Carter led them inside the apartment which, although Spartan in its furnishings, was actually a large space.

"Most of these are meeting rooms and offices. There are only two bedrooms and I'm using one of them. You can have this room." He opened the door to a small rectangular room. There was nothing inside but a double bed and dresser. "The other room available is an office but it has a pullout couch. I've been told it's quite comfortable."

"Thank you."

Carter left him to take care of Tabitha. He laid her atop the bed facedown. She was already asleep.

Rory returned to his car for his overnight bag and portable workstation. He followed Carter with his things to the office with the sofa bed…on the opposite side of the apartment. He preferred something nearer Tabitha but this would have to do. It was a safe house, after all.

"The only bathroom is just down the hall." Carter pointed to a door on the left. "There's a linen closet inside with what you might need. Even clothing. Anything I should know before I log you into the database and go to bed myself?"

"Oh, right." Rory sighed. "You got my badge number from Stroop?"

Carter nodded. "The woman?"

"Ms. Tabitha Beaumont. She's hiding from a hit man named Victor DeWitt. I'm searching for her brother, Dr. Maxwell Beaumont, resident of Richmond. He's wanted for questioning in the Henly murder."

Carter made a face. "Nice family. Good night, Farrell."

"Good night, Carter."

Rory watched the young agent walk away and slip into another room near the front of the apartment. Rory entered his own room, grabbed his bag and headed to the bath. He showered, shaved and slipped into a pair of Levi's. Cleaner and much more comfortable, he set up his computer in the room and contacted his team. There wasn't anything new for him to work with. So, he logged out and started to unfold the sofa bed. His cell buzzed across the table where he'd left it.

"Farrell."

"That's a very pretty lady you're with, Special Agent."

Rory fell silent at the sound of the strange voice. It wasn't DeWitt. DeWitt sounded rougher. This voice was smoother. Refined. Calm. Someone else after Tabitha? Rory's mind swirled with a million emotions, mostly anger.

"Oh, come on, Agent. At least say hello."

Rory swallowed back the bile that had crept up his throat. "What do you want?"

"I want the same thing you want. The nanobullet. And you're going to lead me right to it."

"And why would I do a foolish thing like that?"

"Because if you don't, I'm going to take that sweet thing sleeping with you in the safe house and show her what a real man can do."

This guy was watching them? Rory dropped below the level of the window behind him. He crept to the switch plate and turned off the lights. "Who is this?"

"Anderson Fenton, who else? DeWitt has muffed this up for the last time. I'll be stepping in now."

Fenton. Of course. The arms dealer wasn't just back in the States. He appeared to be right across the street. It made sense—there was a lot riding on this for him. If he had Henly's technology, the nanobullet would be available to every terrorist who could afford it. The nanobullet was, literally, worth a fortune to Fenton.

"Well," Fenton continued, "I can tell I've left you speechless. And you know I have to hang up just in case you were smart enough to trace the call. So, sleep tight. And remember. I'm counting on you." The line went dead.

Rory hit Redial. The number on the screen had been blocked and the function failed. He called Jameson to see what he could do. Then he called Stroop.

"Stay where you are. He obviously wants you to move," his boss said. "I'll send some lookouts and position them around the block. You get some sleep."

"Yeah. I'll try."

"Get some sleep. That's an order."

Rory clicked off. His heart still raced from the threatening phone call, but Stroop's idea sounded good. He needed to recharge. However, this room was too far from Tabitha. He was a heavy sleeper—that might be a good trait for a marine, but it was a bad one for a bodyguard.

He crept down the corridor leading to her room, his mind still on the case. He already dreaded telling her that her brother's car had been found and not her brother. And now, this phone call. They needed to find Max and fast. Max was the key to this case. Or was he?

Too many of her brother's actions made no sense. It was hard to understand why, if he'd known his sister was in danger, he hadn't done something more to ensure her safety. Why, on Monday, did he meet Henly again?

Rory stood in the open doorway looking at Tabitha as the soft light from the hallway fell over her. Why had DeWitt come after her again? Knowing that Fenton was behind all of this—it made the danger she was in that much deeper.

How did Fenton know their location? Had he been at Max's with DeWitt? Did he follow them? Rory shook his head. He was so tired his head had fallen to his chest twice. No more clear thinking could be done.

Rory moved beside Tabitha's bed. She slept hard. It didn't appear she'd moved since he'd left her. He found an afghan at her feet and covered her. Looking down at her soft face, he experienced that little jolt she gave him. He laughed at himself.

*Son, when you finally fall, you're going to fall hard* his father had said many times before he'd become ill.

"You were right, Pop," Rory whispered into the darkness. "And I have almost no chance of her loving me back. She's been through so much and I don't think she trusts me. Funny thing is, I don't care. I love her, anyway. I think I helped her today and it made me feel so good I wanted to burst. I'm fairly certain she's going to break my heart. But it doesn't matter. I finally understand how you felt about Mom. I'm sorry she never came back to you. To us."

Rory sighed, not bothering to wipe the single tear that slid down his cheek. He wished more than ever that he could really talk to his father. But for the first time in months, he didn't feel lonely. He had Tabitha in his life and God to thank for her.

He reached down with one hand and gently brushed the loose curls away from her face, exposing her smooth olive skin. *Thank You for this woman. Thank You for her guiding me back to You.*

Kneeling beside her, he leaned in and kissed her soft skin.

"You smell good," she whispered. Her nose crinkled as she sniffed at him.

"Thanks," he said, his fingers still combing through her long tresses. "If it's okay with you, I'm going to sleep on the floor outside your room. I don't want to leave you alone."

"Too hard," she murmured.

"I'm a marine. I'm used to sleeping on hard floors," he said softly to her ear then brushed a kiss over it.

Her lips curved up in amusement and, he hoped, contentment. For one brief second, he imagined himself in that bed curled up beside her as her husband.

"You're a hopeful fool," he chided himself, reaching for the spare pillow.

Rory stretched his length over the hardwood floor just outside Tabitha's room, remembering a couple of nights in the marine corps when he'd slept on bare concrete. This felt like a feather bed compared to that. Fenton's voice rattled through his thoughts as he drifted to sleep.

# EIGHTEEN

Tabitha awoke with a start. The white walls of an unfamiliar room surrounded her, its paint cracked and chipped. Under her was a soft bed covered with a gray spread that had seen better days. The faint smell of tobacco smoke and old wood hung in the air.

Tabitha pressed herself up, but the sudden movement sent a swift ache rippling through her back and hands. She fell back to the mattress. The events of the previous night returned to her in a rush of dark images—the dental office, the broken glass, Victor DeWitt. The thought of his stinking breath huffing across her neck sent a shiver through her.

She wiggled her sore body to the edge of the bed and willed her feet over the side. Slowly, she transferred her weight to her legs then shuffled to the door, trying to remember where the bathroom was. She'd been so out of it when she'd come in last night, she didn't remember.

Tabitha stopped at the door, vaguely recalling Rory's words to her about sleeping nearby. And there he was, stretched over the hardwood in jeans and a T-shirt. He looked surprisingly content. Peaceful. Handsome.

A smile crossed her tired-looking face.

Yesterday, she'd felt so embarrassed, uncomfortable, even angry with him for pressing into her business the way he had. But she'd needed it. She'd had no idea how much anger had buried itself in her heart, deep beneath that phony front she put on for everyone. Forcing her to confront her fear had been a release and a revelation.

*Lord, I built a wall between me and my pain, my family and friends. Even between me and You. I thought I was dealing with things. I said the words and prayed the prayers but I didn't allow You to heal me. I've been trying to control every aspect of my life. Forgive me and thank You for Your patience. I know I have a lot to work through. But from now on, I want You in control. Not me.*

Tabitha felt a peace and calm in her soul she hadn't experienced in some time. She felt promise in the day to come. Today, they would find her brother. Today, this nightmare would be over. Today and every day God would rule her mind and her heart.

Her heart? Tabitha glanced over at Rory still deep in slumber. She wasn't going to lie to herself anymore, pretend that she could ignore what she felt for him. Over the past five days, this man had stormed his way into her life and stripped away the thick layers that protected her heart.

She took a long, deep breath. Giving her control to God was one thing. Putting her heart on the line for a man was another. And something to think about another day.

Now, for that bathroom. She slid around his legs and out into the hallway. His hand reached up and snatched her ankle. She gasped at his sudden movement.

"Mornin'," he greeted her, opening one eye. "How are you feeling?"

"A little tender, but I think once I get moving I'll be fine." She straightened her torso and flinched at her soreness. "Ouch. And maybe a couple of aspirins wouldn't hurt. How about you?"

"I'm well." He sat up slowly and stretched, his tight muscles rippling under his shirt.

"You should have slept in a bed, Rory. You're going to be as sore as I am."

"I slept where I wanted to." He paused and smiled. "Well, almost where I wanted to." He winked mischievously.

Tabitha felt herself blushing hard as Rory stood before her. For a moment, he seemed to enjoy her new color. Then he shook his head and frowned. "I'm sorry. That was a bad joke."

Tabitha's eyes went wide. "So, it was a joke? I wasn't sure."

He shot her a crooked smile and leaned against the wall so that they stood shoulder to shoulder. "Yep. You may as well know. I'm hopelessly old-fashioned about such things."

"Me, too." She blushed harder, keeping her eyes on her toes spread wide over the dark hardwood floor. The more she learned about Rory the more she liked him. He was a man of purpose and honor, one with morals and faith. She turned her head to him and gave him a serious look. "I find it hard to believe you don't have a girlfriend. You do, don't you?"

"Why? Are you interested in the job?" His grin widened while the blue of his eyes worked their magic on her.

She laughed. "No. I don't date. I'm not ready yet. I was just curious."

Rory rubbed the back of his neck and stared at the space of white wall across from them. "I haven't dated in a while, either. However, I was engaged years ago."

"Really? What happened?"

He sighed. "It was before one of my deployments to Iraq. I asked this girl I'd been seeing. Then I was gone for nine months. And when I came back, she'd made other plans."

"Ouch."

He scrunched up his nose. "Not really. She did me a favor. I was going to break it off myself. I didn't want to marry her."

Tabitha tilted her head. "You didn't love her or you're not the settling-down type?"

"I didn't love her. Not in the forever-for-the-rest-of-my-life kind of way."

"So why did you ask her?"

Rory shrugged. "It was my first deployment. I was young."

"And since then?"

Rory pushed off the wall and stood in front of her again, his eyes twinkling. "I've been very careful."

"Meaning?"

"I haven't dated much. The truth of it is, my job doesn't really give me the time it requires. But I'm hoping to change some of that… Now that I have my eye on someone."

She frowned. "I thought you said you weren't seeing anyone?"

"New prospect." He touched the tip of his finger to the end of her nose. "Very new."

Tabitha felt the color flood into her face again. "You mean me?" she asked candidly.

"Of course I mean you." He reached out and took her hand. A wave of heat rolled through her—as if her entire body might explode from the touch of his fingers connecting with her own.

Too much. He made her feel too much. Tabitha wasn't ready for this. "I don't know if I'm a wise pick right now."

Rory searched deep into her eyes. "I'm not going to push you."

Tabitha threw her head back. "Ha. Who are you kidding? Pushy is your middle name."

He squeezed her hand and pulled her toward him, until his forehead touched hers. "Actually, my middle name is Edward. Now, go get cleaned up. It will make you feel better."

She looked down at her tattered clothes. "Oh, dear. I must look a sight."

"A sight I wouldn't mind waking up to again and again," he whispered.

"But you're not being pushy?" She lifted an eyebrow.

"Nope. I would never be pushy about love." He pulled her again, but this time behind himself and down the long hallway.

*Love?* Tabitha felt the blood drain from her face.

Rory led her to the other side of the apartment. "Here's the bath. There are some clothes you can borrow in the closet. Help yourself. I'll see if I can get some coffee going." His expression darkened. "I have some news."

The change of subject brought a twinge of guilt to Tabitha. How could she flirt at such a time? Her focus should be on finding Max and nothing else. "No. If you know something about my brother, I want to know now."

Rory's shoulders dropped. "My team found his car."

Tears pooled in her eyes. "And Max?"

"No. They didn't find your brother." He shook his head. "Don't jump to conclusions. Get yourself comfortable and we'll discuss it."

Annoyed, she hobbled through the bathroom door. Rory had more to tell her but for some reason, he liked to dole out his information in bite-size tidbits, making her feel helpless and dependent. It drove her crazy. Everything about him drove her crazy.

"We'll find him," he called after her. "I promise."

She nodded. Sure, they would find him. But would it be too late? Tabitha closed and locked the bathroom door, wishing she could just as easily shut out her doubts and fears.

She turned to the old-fashioned tub and shower, realizing she couldn't bathe without getting her cuts and wounds wet. She started the water running anyway.

Her hands trembled searching the cabinets for an extra toothbrush and towel. She located the clothes Rory had mentioned—among the small pile she found a T-shirt and pair of khaki shorts that might fit. One glance at her reflection confirmed she wasn't holding together as well as she'd thought. Despite the sleep, her eyes looked dark and sunken.

The morning's news hadn't helped. It had only raised more questions. Had Max abandoned his car? Been taken from it? There was something Rory wasn't sharing and that made Tabitha more nervous than ever.

She wanted to trust Rory. She really did. She had to depend on him either way. How much better it would be if there was trust. Especially when he hinted at having something more than a friendship. For that to develop there *had* to be trust.

Hanging her head over the side of the old porcelain tub, Tabitha shampooed her hair without wetting her back and cuts too much. She had to admit she felt better.

The borrowed clothing was a bit large, but fortunately, with the drawstring waistband, she was able to make do. She combed through her long, thick locks and took a look at herself in the mirror, half laughing at the result. She wouldn't win any fashion awards, but at least she had something clean and blood-free to wear. She opened the bathroom door and headed to the foyer.

Rory waited there, gun holstered, cell and pager clipped to his waist; he looked ready for action. His T-shirt had been replaced with a nicely starched, light blue dress shirt. He'd rolled the sleeves up to battle the August humidity. He looked good. Too good. Tabitha frowned and shook her head.

"What?" Rory asked after her expression.

"I'm really tired of you dressing better than me." She smirked.

"What are you talking about? You look nice."

"No. You look nice. I look…" She glanced down at her baggy clothing. "Silly."

He chuckled and touched her cheek.

Tabitha looked around for the coffee he'd promised. "Are we leaving? Where's the coffee?"

"We're going out for coffee. Our man Carter is caffeine-free."

"Are you serious? A caffeine-free cop? Never heard of such a thing."

"That's what I was thinking." Rory opened the front door and waved goodbye to Carter, who had apparently been listening to their conversation. "Any place around here for a good strong brew?"

Tabitha headed through the open door. "You're in luck. We're one block from a college campus. There's nothing *but* coffee places. I'll take you to my favorite. I think they have doughnuts, too."

"Cute," he said, following her out.

Tabitha led the way down the tree-covered sidewalks. The city streets bubbled with morning commuters, joggers and students heading to class. In less than five minutes, they reached a mom-and-pop coffee and pastry shop called Uni-Perk-Sity.

She ordered plain coffee and a wheat bagel. Rory took the same, paid and led her to a small table at the front of the store.

"Okay. Out with it, Rory. What do you know? Why aren't we talking in the safe house?"

He scratched his head and leaned over the small table. "I didn't want to talk there."

She made a goofy face and whispered in a mocking tone. "You think Carter is an informant? I think you need a vacation, Agent Farrell."

"Don't knock Carter. He's a newbie, but he's got a perfectly good pair of ears. We couldn't risk talking there."

Tabitha pressed her brows together. "I thought that was a safe house. What's going on? You're making me very nervous."

"Don't be. See that man across the street in the blue shorts and red cap? And, over there, that blond lady taking a seat on the patio with the newspaper?"

She nodded.

"They're protecting you," Rory continued. "You don't need to be afraid."

"The fact that I need cover is enough to terrify me. Where is Max?"

"Slow down, Tabitha." Rory took a few sips from his coffee. "Eat some breakfast and I'll explain what I'm thinking."

Tabitha smeared cream cheese on her bagel and watched Rory eat his in three quick bites.

"Last night, Detective Marks and the Charlotte PD forfeited your case to the FBI," he said. "That's not unusual. When they came up with Victor DeWitt as a suspect, it's not surprising the FBI would want to lead the investigation. But they don't have the Henly case to connect to it. From the very first attack, DeWitt thought you or your brother had something that he wanted, right?"

"Right. But I don't know what he wants. I don't have anything."

"Well, there are two things missing from Henly's apartment—the Vasloh painting and a storage device. We know where the artwork is…so I think DeWitt is looking for this USB storage device with Henly's work on it."

Her stomach started to turn. The combination of strong coffee and touchy conversation wasn't setting well. "Rory, this isn't making me feel better. Are you suggesting Max killed Roger for this flash drive? And that DeWitt is trying to grab me as bait to get the device from Max?"

"No. I don't think that at all. I don't think your brother killed Henly. I think a man named Fenton did."

"Fenton? Does he work for DeWitt?" Tabitha asked.

"It's the other way around. DeWitt and that man O'Conner who drives for him, they work for Fenton."

"So where is this Fenton person? Does he have Max?" Tabitha could feel her pulse pounding in her neck and temples.

Rory cleared his throat and gave her a serious look that affected her to the pit of her stomach. "No. He doesn't have Max. But he wants the device. He thinks you'll lead him to it. I don't know exactly how, but he's been watching us."

Her hands began to tremble. "What do you mean 'watching us'?"

"Fenton called me last night. He knew where we were, that you were asleep at the safe house."

"That's why you slept in the hall?"

He nodded.

"Why didn't we just go somewhere else?" Tabitha asked.

Rory shook his head. "Because that's what he wanted us to do."

"What will happen when these people realize I don't have anything?"

Rory reached out and covered her hand with his own. "It's not going to get that far. We'll find your brother and end this. I just wanted you to know that there has been another complication."

Tabitha emitted a hysterical laugh. "You call that a *complication?*"

"The fact that Fenton phoned means he feels pressed. That can work to our advantage."

"Okay. But how will you find my brother? And what if I'm right, Rory? What if we find Max and he's had nothing to do with this? Then what?"

Rory sighed. "At this point that doesn't really matter. DeWitt and Fenton think you or maybe Max have this storage device. And they will keep trying to get you until they get what they want."

"Great." Tabitha leaned over the table. "So, what's on this storage device anyway?"

Rory's lips went flat. Obviously, he couldn't tell her. She wondered what else he was keeping from her.

"Well, you can't keep me from guessing," she said. "Some sort of files, obviously. I know Roger made weapons. Oh, oh. A bullet. The word *bullet* on the mirror."

She noticed the slight change in Rory's expression.

"That's it, isn't it?" she asked. "Roger made some kind of special bullet."

"Are you sure you wouldn't consider a career change?" He smirked. "You're really good at this."

Tabitha gave one definitive shake of her head. "No way. I'll keep my boring worker's comp gig… What's so special about Roger's bullet? Or do I want to know?"

"It's a nanobullet. It never misses. Fenton is an illegal arms dealer. So imagine the concern here."

Tabitha closed her eyes. "What was Roger thinking?"

"Well, he was thinking millions of dollars when he agreed to the deal," Rory mumbled. "But either he had a change of heart or he wanted more money. Probably the latter. I think that's why he stored the details for the technology on this one certain device and then erased all other copies. Most likely, he was supposed to hand the files over last week to Fenton. But he didn't."

"It still doesn't explain why these people are after me and Max," Tabitha stated.

"I'm hoping your brother can do that."

Tabitha leaned back in her seat. "Well, no way Max helped Roger with this. Max didn't believe in Roger's work. He wouldn't have helped Roger do anything with it."

"I'm not saying your brother agreed to anything, Tabitha."

Her face flushed with anger at the direction the conversation seemed to have taken. "Then what *are* you saying? I don't have anything and I'm sure Max doesn't, either."

"No. You don't *think* you have anything. We can't rule out that you might have a copy of that technology and don't even know it."

"How? That's ridiculous." Tabitha clenched her teeth.

"Is it?" he asked.

She felt her cheeks burning. "How can you even suggest such a thing? I haven't been in the same city as Roger for two years. The only way I could have anything from him is if Max agreed to help him and then planted something on me himself."

When Rory didn't correct her statement, she knew he was actually considering the preposterous scenario.

"I knew it! You still believe Max was in on this. Every time I think I can trust you, you remind me why I shouldn't. We're not on the same side." Tabitha stood abruptly and started for the door.

Rory grabbed her hand. "Don't walk out of here. Don't make a scene. Please. Sit down and listen to me." His voice sounded smooth and low.

"You know, I don't think my own father ever bossed me around like you do." In her dictionary, the term *bully* had a new definition—Rory Edward Farrell.

"I admit sometimes I can be overbearing. But this is for your own protection, I promise. Now, sit down." His voice remained calm and steady.

She reluctantly returned to her seat, but turned her head to look out the front window, away from him. She didn't know what was more annoying—his commanding words or the fact that she'd obeyed them.

"We are absolutely on the same side," he whispered. "Tabitha, face the facts. Somehow, you and your brother are involved in this mess. Only your brother can tell us if he was a willing participant or not. I know you were not. I want to find your brother and make sure he has the chance to tell us his side of things. I want to believe you. I want to believe that your trust in Max is well-placed."

Her anger abated somewhat. "So, what now? You think that drive was hidden behind the painting?"

"No. I checked it last night. The back of the canvas doesn't look touched. I don't think the drive was ever there. The more I think about it, the more I believe the Vasloh was a payoff or just what Henly said it was—a gift."

"A payoff?" She made a face at him, disappointed that he kept referring to the possibility of Max's guilt.

"Okay. You're right," he said. "I can't *prove* any of these things. Right now I can't *prove* that your case and Henly's are even related. But I can certainly speculate. Stop reasoning like a lawyer for one second and put together what you know."

"Okay, but how does all this speculating help us to find Max?"

"I think your brother has been picked up."

"Picked up?" she repeated.

Rory nodded. "Yes, by the FBI."

"Arrested?"

His eyes rolled at her. "Not arrested. Picked up. He could have gone to them with what he knew."

Tabitha sat back and soaked in this theory. She had to admit she liked the idea. It meant Max was safe. Not with DeWitt or this Fenton person. And not dead. "Well, wouldn't you be able to find out if he was in custody?"

Rory shook his head. "Not necessarily. The FBI doesn't have to disclose the whereabouts of someone in protective custody."

Tabitha slumped in her chair. "Then…you're just guessing?"

"Yes. I'm guessing. Would you give me a break here? I'm pretty good at this stuff."

"All right." She waved her hands in the air. "Let's just say for one second that I buy into this explanation of yours. What do we do now?"

"We need to go back to the safe house. Let me see what I can dig up. I might have to misdirect Carter on a few things. All you have to do is follow my lead."

"What else is new?" She smirked and followed him out of the coffee shop.


At the safe house, Rory contacted his team while Tabitha phoned her office and then Sasha.

"Finally, you call me," her roommate said in a scolding tone. "Did you find Max?"

"No," Tabitha responded. "But I found Agent Farrell."

"You called him?" Sasha said with excitement.

"More like he showed up at Max's house right after I did."

"Ah. He found you. And what about your brother? Any leads?"

"Maybe." Tabitha swallowed hard, afraid to say more. "Let's talk about you. What are you doing?"

"Cleaning our house," Sasha said. "The FBI agents said I could get started."

"Sasha, don't do that all by yourself. Wait until I get back."

"And when is that gonna be?"

"I—I don't know. When we find Max."

"He's in a lot of trouble, isn't he?"

"Roger is dead." Tabitha heard her voice quiver with the words.

"Oh, dear, girl. Where are ya? I want to come and help."

"Thanks, Sasha. But you can't. I'll call you tomorrow."

"Yeah. Well, you can't stop me from praying for ya."

Tabitha pressed the phone hard to her ear, drinking in the strength and encouragement of her friend. "Pray hard, Sasha. Pray very hard."

Tabitha dialed Karin, too, but there was no answer. Her head started to pound as she rechecked the number and tried again. Voice mail. She left a message then called information for a number to the Gill estate. It was unlisted.

Rory walked into her room with a quick gait. "Ready to go?"

"Did you find—" She swallowed down the rest of the question since Rory's expression made it clear she should not continue. This cloak-and-dagger act had her insides scrambled. "I'm ready," she whispered.

Rory reached his hand out and led her to the front of the apartment. They thanked Carter and told him they were headed to NCIS headquarters. Tabitha wondered if that was the truth. They exited the building and walked straight to Rory's car without uttering a word to one another.

Tabitha settled with care into the passenger seat. The effects of the aspirins she'd taken had started to wear off, the stiffness returning. Rory climbed in, closed the door and cranked the engine. In less than five minutes, they were headed north on I-95 toward DC.

"Are we really going to your headquarters?" she asked.

Rory shook his head. "Let's stop for breakfast."

"Breakfast? We just had—"

Rory placed a hand on her arm.

"Yes, I'm really hungry," she said.

Rory removed his hand. The corners of his lips curled up. He obviously had no idea how helpless and scared she felt.

They pulled off the highway and parked in the lot of a busy pancake house. Rory took her by the arm and leaned close as they walked inside.

"We're changing cars," he whispered. "Just in case Fenton is following."

Tabitha frowned. She'd thought knowing what they were doing would calm her but the blatant reminder of her dangerous situation was no comfort at all. "Karin didn't answer her phone this morning," she whispered back.

"She's probably sleeping. We'll try her again. She's well protected where she is. Let's just worry about one thing at a time."

They drank an orange juice at a booth in the back of the restaurant. When the waitress put the bill down, there was a car key next to it.

Rory slid the key into his palm and they left through an exit next to the bathroom. Outside, an old Chevrolet was parked in a loading zone.

"This is like something out of a bad espionage movie," she grumbled.

"It's a precaution we need to take." Rory turned their replacement vehicle onto Route 1 back toward town. "We can talk freely now."

"Are we going to Max?" she asked hopefully.

"One more change then my boss will tell us where to go."

Hope surged through her body. "You found him."

"He's been picked up, but the FBI isn't playing nice. They won't give us a location. My boss has gone to the Secretary of Defense."

Tabitha slumped down in the passenger seat.

"Have a little faith," Rory said. He looked over and gave her a wink.

From Route 1, Rory pulled into a large shopping complex

and parked. He led her through a department store where they picked up a package at Customer Service. Inside the package was another car key. They exited the store through an "Employee Only" entrance and loaded themselves into a shiny, new Cadillac Seville.

"Open the glove compartment," he told her.

Inside, Tabitha found a small cell phone.

"Press Redial."

With shaky fingers, she hit the redial button. Max picked up on the second ring.

# NINETEEN

"Max!" Tabitha's face lit with complete joy the second her brother picked up. It made yanking the phone out her hands feel terribly cruel. But Rory couldn't blow his one and only chance of finding out where Max was. Especially not when Stroop had pulled some serious strings to get this call placed.

Rory pressed the phone to his ear. "This is NCIS Special Agent Farrell. I need to speak with the Special Agent in Charge."

Tabitha's angry grimace made his heart sink to his stomach. For a moment, he wondered why he was even doing this. He'd always been good at switching off emotions while working a case, but with Tabitha that had become impossible. Maybe he should have called in another agent to look for Max and escorted her to NCIS headquarters. Especially after that call from Fenton. Was he putting her in danger just because he selfishly wanted to keep her close?

Muffled swears sounded over the line then a strong male voice spoke. A familiar one. "Hello, Captain Farrell."

Pat Hausser, Special Agent in Charge of the Charlotte Field Office, the man he'd just seen earlier that week, was on the line. What was *he* doing with Tabitha's brother? Just how involved were Hausser and the FBI in this mixed-up case with DeWitt and Fenton and Tabitha and her brother?

"I agreed to one phone call from the sister," Hausser continued. "I did not agree to talk to you."

"No, sir." Rory cleared his dry throat. "You did not, but here I am. I don't want to interfere with your case. I just want to interrogate Dr. Max Beaumont. We're on a secure line. Please give his location."

"Son, my instructions were for you to wait until I send for you and Ms. Beaumont."

"I'm sorry, sir, I don't have time to wait. I need to speak with Dr. Beaumont. Now." He looked away from Tabitha, not wanting to witness the disappointed look on her face.

Agent Hausser paused. More muffled cursing sounded. "The Beaumont residence," he said.

Rory's mind swirled in a mad fit as he drove Tabitha back to Max and Karin's home. Had Hausser found Max because of the message on Tabitha's mirror? His team supposedly had taken the case, but why all the secrecy? It made no sense. Why not bring in Tabitha? Hopefully Hausser would explain when they arrived at Max's home.

He reached over and gave Tabitha's hand a squeeze as he parked the Cadillac under the front portico of the big two-story brick home. Tabitha jumped out of the car before he killed the engine.

"Max!" She ran to the man who opened the front door.

Rory watched the reunion, noting that Tabitha and Max Beaumont shared the same large brown eyes and nice, wide smile. Physically, however, they looked very different. Max had a thick, broad build where Tabitha's frame stretched long and lean. Rory stood back for a moment, enjoying the look of relief on Tabitha's tired face.

Her brother appeared equally exhausted. Stress showed in the dark circles under his eyes and the pronounced worry lines across his brow. "Tabs, I'm so sorry about all this," he apologized.

She hugged him again as Karin appeared at the front door. Hoover scooted between her legs and out toward the yard. Rory grabbed him by the neck and carried him back.

"Agent Farrell." Max reached a hand to him. "Thank you for keeping my sister safe and for getting Karin back to her father."

Rory shook his hand and then Karin's.

"I just got here myself," she said.

Max nodded, putting his arm around his wife. "I finally convinced them that Karin would hire a search posse if I continued to ignore her calls."

Rory followed the Beaumonts into the study, where they found Hausser sitting at Karin's large mahogany desk. Judging by his stiff greeting, he wasn't pleased with their presence. Rory turned to an operations table his people had set in the corner and introduced his two-man team.

"Special Agent Farrell, this is FBI Special Agent Sutton and DEA Special Agent Reams."

Rory shook their hands, lifting a brow at the DEA's presence. Was it possible Hausser was working a completely separate case? He noticed Max rolling his eyes at the whole scene then pulling Tabitha and Karin away to the kitchen. Hoover lagged behind them with his nose to the ground. At Hausser's cue, Agent Sutton followed the family. The SAC wouldn't give them five minutes in private. Rory dropped his head in disappointment. Before, he'd admired Hausser's leadership abilities. Today he was seriously questioning them.

Hausser crossed his arms over his chest. "You don't get the dentist until this afternoon. I've cleared that with both our directors. Feel free to check if you want."

"That's not necessary." Rory tried to hide his growing irritation. "Can I at least ask him a few questions?"

Hausser gestured to the kitchen. "Knock yourself out. Agent Sutton stays put."

"Anything I should know about why you picked up Beaumont?" Rory asked.

"Vicodin. Lots and lots of Vicodin," the SAC replied with a smug air.

"You're pressing drug charges on Dr. Beaumont?" Rory

wanted to laugh. He was working a case that threatened the nation's security and Hausser was squabbling for Beaumont over some prescription drugs?

"It's unclear the level of Beaumont's participation. There are other dentists and doctors involved. Beaumont has agreed to help us operate a sting this afternoon."

That explained why the DEA was there. But why whisk Beaumont away from his family? Seemed like overkill.

"You have an undercover?" Rory asked, suspicious of such a small team.

"That's enough questions, Farrell. You don't work for me yet." Hausser's tone was threatening.

Rory walked away, shaking his head. Was Hausser even working Tabitha's case? It sure didn't seem like a priority. Rory entered the kitchen, where Agent Sutton, a thin, freckle-faced man of maybe twenty-three, had taken a seat at a bar stool. Rory joined him and made some small talk so that Tabitha, Karin and Max could finish speaking in relative privacy on the other side of the room.

After a few minutes, Karin and then Tabitha excused themselves. Rory sensed how difficult this must be for Tabitha. Not only had Max been caught up in this mess with Henly, now he and his dental office were being investigated for drugs.

Max came over to the bar where Rory sat with Agent Sutton and leaned over the counter. "Tabitha doesn't like the deal I made."

"Which deal is that?" Rory asked. "The one you made with the FBI to save your practice or the one you made with Henly to get rich off his nanodevice?" Rory studied Max's eyes, ready to judge his reaction.

The dentist shook his head. "That doesn't deserve a response. But because you helped my wife and my sister—and by the way, I want them both out of here—I'm going to tell you the same thing I told the others."

"I'm not interested in the drugs," Rory said. "Just Henly. You

do know about his—" One look at Max's face showed he'd
heard of his friend's death.

"I saw the news last night." Max glanced away for a second
with his teeth clenched, then looked back. It wasn't grief
exactly, but some kind of regret showed in his long expression.

"I just want the truth," Rory declared.

Max looked doubtfully toward Agent Sutton.

"He needs to stay. But it's just me and you talking," Rory
stated.

Max exhaled heavily and rubbed his eyes. "Henly? Where
do I start?"

"Start at the beginning," Rory said. "When did he tell you
about the nanobullet?"

Max's eyes went wide. "Is that what he was selling? A
bullet?"

"Talk, Beaumont. Hausser's only going to give us so much
time."

Max nodded. "Yeah, so…Henly threw me a huge bachelor
party about a month before the wedding. After he'd had a few
drinks, he told me about some killer weapon he'd developed
and how much he could get for it if he sold it to the 'right'
people. He said I needed in on it so that I could keep Karin
living in style. He said it'd be just like we'd planned when we
were kids. Both of us rich with gorgeous women.

"I couldn't believe it. I mean, Roger was always crossing
lines, you know. That's what made him fun to hang out with.
You never knew what he would do next. But it was always
harmless stuff before. This was…way over. Beyond anything
he'd ever suggested.

"So, of course, I said no. But he thought I was crazy not to
want in on it. He got furious with me. Kept insisting. Saying
that all I had to do was keep this storage device while he
bartered for some more money. He even laughed and said I was
perfect for the job because I wouldn't understand what was on
the device even if I could figure out how to download it.

"I was sad for him. Henly could have done something really great with his genius. Instead, he let it turn him into a criminal.

"Anyway," Max continued, "I didn't see him or hear from him for a couple of months, which isn't unusual. We stay in touch but it's sporadic. He was out of the country during my wedding. Then last week, he calls out of the blue and says he has my wedding gift. Asks if I'll meet him for lunch and pick up the gift. I thought 'Sure. Why not?' I'd hoped maybe he'd gotten some sense back into his head.

"So, last Friday, I met him at Stone Grill. Roger showed up late and drunk. I wanted to leave but I was afraid he'd try to drive home in that condition. So I stayed. He talked crazy the whole time. Kept saying he was so glad I changed my mind and that he had something really sweet for my efforts. I just blew it off. I mean, he was really drunk. I decided that he'd finally crossed that line. You know, the one between genius and madness.

"After lunch, I drove him home. He insisted that I take that Vasloh. I just wanted out of there. I helped him wrap up the painting. I made some coffee for him, hoping he'd sober up. Then I left."

"And that's it?" Rory asked. So far, everything Max said went along with Henly's timeline. Just as convincingly, his body language, eye contact, even the tone of his voice denoted he told the truth. "He never specifically asked you about the USB device? Or about your sister?"

"No. He said nothing about a storage drive. And…well…he always talks about Tabs." Max rolled his eyes.

"Think hard," Rory urged. "What did he say about your sister? It's important," Rory demanded.

"Come on. He was drunk. He said the usual stuff about her. You know, stuff a brother doesn't want to hear." Max shook his head. "He did say something strange. I mean, it wasn't about Tabitha exactly, and I didn't put the pieces together at the time. But—" He ran his fingers through his hair and gave a half chuckle. "I'm so dense. At the restaurant, he asked me if Tabitha still had 'it.' I thought he was talking about the football."

"The football?" Rory repeated, lifting an eyebrow curiously.

Tabitha reappeared in the kitchen doorway, looking upset and a little guilty for eavesdropping. She walked over and planted herself next to Max, crossing her arms over her chest.

"It's a football signed by Joe Montana," she said matter-of-factly. "Roger gave it to us years ago. Max and I share custody. This year, I have it, although now it's slashed to pieces—like everything else in my house." She looked back at her brother as if he'd slayed her. "You told him I had it, didn't you?"

"I'm sorry. I had no idea, Tabitha. Not until you called me Sunday night and then I knew Roger had somehow involved us in this. But I still don't know how. I've been racking my brain over it and—"

"What happened on Monday?" Rory interrupted.

"Well, I didn't sleep Sunday night. I kept thinking about what happened to Tabs. I went into the office and tried to work, but I couldn't focus. So, I decided I would go to Charlotte whether Tabitha wanted me to or not. I told Karin enough to get her to go to her dad's beach house. Then I canceled patient appointments, but as I was leaving town, Roger called. I guess it was from a pay phone because I didn't recognize the number. I almost didn't answer. Anyway, Roger said he needs the device back. That his bluff wasn't working. That they were going to kill him. He sounded pitiful. I told him what had happened to Tabitha on the mountain. He said it was all his fault. Everything was his fault. He was crying.

"I know I shouldn't have, but I went to see him. I met Roger at the Stone Grill again. This time he was lucid. But in a mood. Freaking out, actually. We had words. When he finally realized that I did not have the storage device, he left in a panic.

"After that, I'd planned to go to the police. But I barely got out of that restaurant before the FBI and DEA were all over me about drugs in my office." He looked pathetically to his sister. "Agent Hausser told me if I did what he asked he'd keep Karin's name out of it. He promised me that you were safe, too. I didn't know about your break-in. I'm sorry, Tabitha."

She embraced him. The hug looked accepting, but the expression on her face was one of hurt and confusion. Rory's gut tightened. The one man she really trusted in her life had just let her down. It had to hurt.

For Rory, however, Max's story explained several things—most important, why DeWitt had come after Tabitha and why Max hadn't gone straight to the police. "Dr. Beaumont, do you know anything about the device? Or its whereabouts?"

"Nothing. I swear."

"What did Henly say when you told him you didn't have the storage device?" Rory asked.

"I don't know. He was crazy."

"Did you ask Henly why he thought you and Tabitha had the device?"

"Of course I did. But his answer didn't make any sense."

"What did he say?"

"He said…" Max shook his head. "He said we should never trust the people we work with."

Rory wondered if Henly had meant those words for himself or for Max. Either way it was worth checking on. "Is it possible someone overheard you and Henly talking at the bachelor party?"

"I doubt it. We'd gone outside. Roger had a cigar he wanted to smoke. But who knows? It was a huge party. There must have been over fifty people there."

Rory showed Max the picture of DeWitt on his cell phone. "Ever seen this man?"

Max's face went white. "Not at the party. But I saw him at Stone Grill on Friday. He was sitting at a nearby table. Is that who killed…"

"We don't know." Rory ran a hand over his buzz cut,

thinking. "So, could you possibly come up with a list of who attended your bachelor party? I think that would be a good place to start."

"Sure." Max nodded.

Rory left Tabitha and Max to talk while he processed Max's story. Somehow Henly thought that Max had taken him up on the deal and involved Tabitha. If Max was telling the absolute truth, then what they needed was to find the person who had misled Henly. Probably someone from that party.

Rory's thoughts were interrupted as he saw Hausser hustling Max into the study.

"Sir, I need Beaumont to make a list for me," Rory said.

"He can do whatever you want after two o'clock. It's my show until then. We're mobilizing."

Rory shook his head and motioned for Hausser to join him in the hallway. "This is a matter of national security," he whispered. "You're worried about a few cases of Vicodin? Do you see the difference?"

"Look. You've got Beaumont. Your boss is happy. If you want, you're welcome to come along on the bust and keep an eye on the dentist."

"You can't be serious," Rory said.

"The drugs are changing hands today. This is a huge operation. I need two hours. If you don't want to come along, then stay here. It's up to you."

Rory stared at him for a long moment in disbelief. But Hausser wasn't going to bend and he was the one calling the shots. Rory walked away, dialing Stroop's number.

# TWENTY

Stroop was tied up in a meeting with the Director of NCIS and the Director of the FBI, which meant Rory had to decide how to handle the situation with Hausser on his own.

That very minute, Agent Hausser and the team were going over their plan. He could either tag along, with Tabitha at the house under guard, or stay behind and guard her himself. Taking her on the raid was not an option. He never wanted to see her in the line of fire again. She'd be safe at the house. Still, what a choice. Of course, he would have preferred to stay, but that meant leaving Hausser unsupervised and Rory didn't feel that he could. Hausser's presence for this DEA operation seemed unnecessary. There was more to his being here than he was telling Rory, and the best way to figure it out was to stick to Hausser until the situation came to a head.

Rory called in a local detective unit to watch over Tabitha and her sister-in-law. Lieutenant Dillon showed up in less than ten minutes, a stout sandy-haired fellow with a carefully trimmed Fu Manchu.

"Stay together and with Lieutenant Dillon," Rory instructed Tabitha and Karin. The women nodded. They both looked tired and nervous. Rory turned to the detective. "You have a man outside?"

"Yes, sir. My partner is out front." Dillon hurried over to join

Rory. He looked as nervous as Tabitha and Karin, shifting his hands in and out of his pockets.

Rory hated leaving Tabitha. But besides keeping an eye on Hausser, there was another benefit. It separated Max from Tabitha. He didn't know where Fenton was or what he knew but if the man got both Max and Tabitha at the same time, Rory would lose whatever negotiating power he might need to keep them alive. He hoped it wouldn't come down to that, but it was better to plan for the worst.

"If anything spooks you," Rory said to Dillon, "you take both of them into the station." Dillon nodded. Rory stepped up to Tabitha, took her hand in his and pulled her in for a quick kiss. "I'll see you soon."

Tabitha nodded. "Keep Max safe," she whispered.

Rory pulled himself away and strode out of the house. *Lord, please keep her safe. Keep her—*

"Here," Agent Reams interrupted his prayer, handing him an earpiece. "Hausser and I will be in the van. We'll park one block down from the dental office in the back alley—behind that furniture store. You'll park across the street at Rick's Subs. Watch the front end of the office. We might need you to tail a suspect, so stay alert."

Rory reached for the earpiece and locked eyes with Agent Reams. Her face looked tight and anxious. Not the expression of an agent certain to close a huge case in the next hour.

*Why are you working with Hausser?* The question burned on the edge of Rory's tongue, but he didn't ask it. He nodded and took the device. Reams turned away and climbed into the van. Rory got into the Cadillac and drove to Rick's Subs. In front of the deli, he angled his car so that he could see the dental office and waited.

Twenty minutes passed. Most of the time, the view of Max's office was blocked by traffic. And the earpiece seemed to send him selective feed. As far as he was concerned, being here was useless. What he really needed was that bachelor party guest list from Max.

Rory called Agent Jameson. "How much longer is Stroop in that meeting?"

"Don't know. Why?" Jameson asked.

"I think Hausser's off on this. I find it hard to believe he got this operation approved. He said for me to check with the directors but there was no time and he probably knew they were in a meeting."

"What are you going to do?"

Rory sighed. "I'm going to wait a little longer and then I'm going to bang on the back door of that van and demand an explanation."

"I don't blame you," Jameson agreed.

"Well, in the meantime, I have a long shot for you."

"A challenge," Jameson said. "Lay it on me."

"Henly gave Beaumont a bachelor party about a month before he married. So I guess that was three months ago. It's when he told Beaumont about the nanobullet. Someone must have overheard. Then blackmailed Henly or stepped in for Max, offering to keep the storage device. Maybe they snatched the storage device. Anyway, we need to check the guest list."

"Sure, man. I'm on it. I'll call you when I get anything."

Rory settled into his car seat, wishing he'd eaten a better breakfast. The smells floating from Rick's Subs were driving his stomach wild and causing his mouth to water.

He continued to watch the front of Max's office. A glass company had arrived to replace the broken front doors as a few of the employees trickled out for lunch. Almost an hour had passed. If Hausser's team was going to do something, he wished they'd get started.

"Michaels is on the move," Agent Reams spoke into the transmitter. "Sutton, you tail him. He's in the red Jeep Commander. Farrell, you watch Elise Jenkins."

Rory pressed the earpiece. "Could I get some specifics?"

There was a long pause before Reams answered. "Negative. Just tail Jenkins."

Rory sighed then started his car. He spotted the gray-headed receptionist climbing into a silver Toyota Camry. Did they really think this little old lady was the mastermind behind a drug operation? Stranger things had happened.

Reams and Hausser had not shared much about the sting operation. Rory knew only that an undercover agent had set up a sale and that they had a couple of suspects from the office. Since the office had to have a dentist on-site to operate, they'd needed Max at work so that Michaels would be free to exit the building. Now, he supposed that Michaels and Elise Jenkins were their suspects.

What was taking so long? It seemed like Rory and her brother had been gone for hours. Tabitha checked her watch. It had been less than an hour. And for the past few minutes, Karin had been on the phone. Leaving her to sit and stare at the walls.

"Let's get away from this room," Tabitha said, as soon as Karin was off the phone. "I'm feeling like a caged animal."

"Right." Karin nodded.

Tabitha and Karin moved from the study into the neighboring den. Lieutenant Dillon followed. Hoover scrambled at their heels, licking the wood floor along the way. As they entered, Tabitha noticed the empty space where the Vasloh had hung the day before.

"What happened to the painting?" Tabitha asked.

"Max and I both agreed that we couldn't stand the sight of it. Maybe we should sell it and give the money to a women's shelter?"

Tabitha smiled. "You told Max?"

"No. There was no time. You can tell him later."

Tabitha fell onto a large slip-covered couch. Karin sat at the other end. The puppy tried to jump between them but couldn't quite reach. He yelped with each effort.

"I should have told Max two years ago. Then we wouldn't all be in this mess," Tabitha mumbled.

"You can't blame yourself for what's happening any more than Max can."

"I should have reported him."

Karin didn't respond.

"Let's talk about something else," Tabitha suggested.

"Like what? The drug bust?" Karin chuckled. "And here I thought I was marrying into this quiet, little academic family."

"I'm glad you're finding humor in this." Tabitha let out a half laugh then turned and stared at Karin. "You are finding humor? Right? You don't think Max is—"

"Of course not. But someone is. Before you got here, Agent Reams told us someone at the dental office has been using phony DEA numbers to double and triple orders of painkillers. They've used suppliers in the U.S., Canada and Mexico. They have the drugs shipped to the office, probably after hours, and then they take them to another location, rebottle them and sell them illegally. There's an undercover agent posing as a buyer. That sale is supposed to take place today at lunch."

"Only Max, Paul and the office manager would know how to use a DEA number."

"Who's the office manager?"

"Elise Jenkins, the receptionist," Tabitha stated.

Karin frowned. Hoover let out a frustrated yelp and again leaped at the sofa.

"You're going to ruin all my furniture, aren't you?" Karin spoke in a baby voice.

"I think he needs to go out," Tabitha said.

"You're right." Karin stood and scooped the puppy into her arms. "Lieutenant?"

Lieutenant Dillon, who'd been standing just outside the doorway, came into the den.

"I need to take the dog out," Karin continued. "Can I let him slip into the back garden?" As she said the words, Hoover wriggled from her arms and escaped to the floor. The puppy ran like mad right through the detective's legs and toward the front of the house, emitting squeaky barks the entire length of his journey.

They all laughed.

"I'll get him." Lieutenant Dillon turned after the dog.

The chimes of the front door echoed through the house.

"And I'll see who that is," he added and walked out of the room.

Tabitha frowned at her sister-in-law, but Karin had moved to the doorway and was calling after the detective. "Watch out, Lieutenant. Hoover likes to run out the front—" Karin shrugged. "I don't think he heard me. I'd better help."

Rory watched Ms. Jenkins pull out of the parking lot and drive right by him into a strip mall. She parked and walked into a nail salon. Rory rolled his eyes. It now occurred to him that Elise Jenkins probably was not a suspect at all. Hausser and Reams might just be giving him something to do to keep him out of the way.

He killed the engine. One more weird call from Hausser and he would do exactly what he'd told Jameson—hunt down Hausser's FBI van and demand some answers.

Rory's cell rang. He reached for it hoping the call was from Stroop. But on the digital display he recognized his grandmother's number. Panic riveted through him. Gram rarely called him. And when she did, she usually had bad news.

"Gram, please tell me you're fine," he pleaded.

"Well, of course I'm fine. Just hadn't heard from you."

His panic mutated to guilt. She was right. He hadn't checked in with her since he'd left Hendersonville. "Sorry, I caught a case before I got back," he explained.

"I figured. Well, I won't keep you. I just wanted to let you know that Mr. Watson and I are getting married next weekend."

*"What?"* Rory sat up fast.

"You heard me," Gram said. "I'm getting married. Come to the wedding if you can."

"Gram, shouldn't you think about this a little more?"

"Oh, Rory, at my age you don't have time to sit around and ponder over these things. The moment will be gone."

Rory let out a little chuckle. "Sorry. I'm just a little shocked, but if this is what you want, then I'm all for it. I wouldn't miss the ceremony. Count me in. I might even bring a date."

"Now that sounds promising. Wouldn't be that lovely young lady I met last weekend, would it?"

"It would."

"Your father would have liked her, Rory."

Rory felt his throat tighten at her words. He missed his dad so much it hurt. "Yeah, I think he would have…" He clenched his teeth. "How do you do it, Gram? How do you get through each day with him gone?"

"The same way I got through each day after your grandfather died. Slowly, but not alone. I have God and I have you. Let go of the anger, Rory. God took your father home early and one day we'll know why. But until then, He wants us to keep living the here and now."

"I'm trying."

"No father could have been prouder. I'm proud of you, too."

"I love you," he said before ending the call.

Rory leaned into the plush leather of the borrowed Cadillac, his mind swirling with fears and doubts. But mixed in there was a budding love for Tabitha and a strong love for his family and friends. Somewhere in all that confusion was a faith and trust in God that needed a little healing from the pain of losing his father.

*God, thank You for my life. It's a good one. You've surrounded me with such wonderful people. I still don't understand why Pop suffered so. Letting go of him has been the most difficult thing. But I accept it. That's what faith is—believing without having every answer. Knowing that You are enough.*

A tear slid down Rory's cheek as he pressed into his seat again. Gram was right. Once this mess with Henly and Fenton was over, he had a lot to look forward to. He needed to live and love, not fester and hide away in his work. It's what his father would have wanted....

He drained a bottle of water he'd stashed in the car and refocused on the case. What was taking Jameson so long to call back? Must have been a really long guest list. If only he could talk to Max.

Rory's thoughts kept falling on Hausser. It didn't feel right that the SAC was so intent on keeping him from Max. Why couldn't he be allowed to work with Max on that guest list inside his office? The entire staff had met him. He'd just been there the day before. Working with Max had nothing to do with this drug bust. Or did it?

Rory shook his head. Hausser's course of actions didn't add up. From what he'd been told, he'd gathered that Reams had worked this case for six months and then Hausser joined her on Monday. Joined? More like took over. Why? It wasn't the type of case that merited his attention. And then they'd picked up Max. Why? Beaumont seemed to know nothing about the drugs. And the timing of it all. Perfect for interfering in the NCIS case. A little too perfect.

Rory's suspicions steamed through his mind. What if his paranoia from Fenton's phone call had been justified? What if Fenton had someone on the inside? Someone to feed him a little information here and there. Someone to let him know what the feds were doing. Someone to help keep him a step ahead. Someone like Hausser.

Or maybe Tabitha was right. Maybe he needed a vacation.

Tabitha. He hoped she was safe. Beaumont's house wasn't a very secure location.

Despite the heat, a chill prickled up his neck. He needed to know that Tabitha was safe. As he reached for his phone, it chimed with a new call.

"Okay. I made a list of Max's male friends." Jameson's voice sounded excited. "Actually, I called his wife and she helped. Then I cross-referenced the list with Henly's recent calls and e-mails. There were four men that came up repeatedly, but one in particular I think you'll find interesting."

"And who's that?"

"Paul Michaels. Just after that party he was in touch with Henly. Four phone calls. And I checked his financials, too. He's got cash. Lots more than his partner."

Yes, Michaels. Rory felt his blood pressure rise. "Thanks, Jameson. I think that's finally enough to stop this crazy drug bust. Inform Stroop when he gets out of that meeting. I'm calling Hausser."

Rory started the car, ready to have a chat with Hausser.

"I…turned…Michaels…right. I…" Agent Sutton's voice broke through blasts of static on the earpiece. The young agent sounded stressed.

Reams asked him to repeat the message.

More static.

"…I lost him."

Sutton had lost Michaels. Perfect.

# TWENTY-ONE

Tabitha stood from her place on the couch and followed Lieutenant Dillon and Karin toward the front door. *Stay together,* Rory had told them.

Lieutenant Dillon looked through the peephole. "I don't see anyone," he said. "But I'll have a look."

Karin caught up to Hoover and put a hand on his collar. Dillon swung the door open and stepped outside. Hoover barked twice and broke away from Karin's hands.

"You little stinker," she yelled after him.

Tabitha could see the frustration in Karin's eyes. "I'll get him," she offered, thinking it would be nice to step into the fresh air for a minute. She took off after the little yellow puppy. Karin followed.

"Back inside, ladies," Dillon ordered.

"Just getting the dog," Tabitha called back without slowing. "Hoover! Here, boy."

Hoover took no notice of her. He seemed on a mission to run as far and as fast as he could. He'd made it to the next yard and showed no signs of stopping. Tabitha let her sandals slip from her feet and kicked herself into high gear. Her body ached from her cuts but she relished the fresh air on her face and the freedom to move, thankful that her ankle had healed.

She caught the puppy at the edge of the neighbor's lawn, tackling him, then turned and jogged back to her brother's home. Passing Dillon's partner who'd jumped from his car at all the action, she gave a quick wave.

"Don't do that again," Dillon warned at the door.

"Me or the dog?" Tabitha smiled and handed Hoover to Karin.

Karin clipped a leash to the dog's collar. "Thanks. I'll go get your shoes."

"No." Dillon stepped in front of the door. "Just leave the shoes. Everyone inside."

"But he still needs to relieve himself," Karin said.

"Fine." Dillon stepped aside. "I'll watch."

Karin moved to the closest grassy area on the lawn.

"I'm going to use a people bathroom," Tabitha announced. She left the foyer and walked the long hall to the powder room. As she passed the study, an arm came around her and pressed a wet cloth deep into her mouth. Another arm encircled her mid-section.

*Oh, Lord. Please no. Not again.*

Tabitha struggled against her attacker. She kicked back and tried to break her arms free, but the man dug his fingers into one of her cuts. The pain was crippling.

"If you don't want to die, then you'll relax and play nice."

Tabitha couldn't quite place the voice, but she knew it. Not DeWitt, but a voice she'd heard before.

With a quick movement, the man released his arm from her waist then pressed something cold and hard into her ribs. A gun.

Tabitha stopped fighting.

"Good little sister. Now out through the kitchen, behind the garage and into my car."

His fingers continued to pinch her open wound as he steered her toward the service alley. The pain made her heave, but somehow she made it behind the neighbor's garage and to the side road where she saw the car. A red Jeep Commander. It was Paul Michaels that held the gun to her back.

\* \* \*

Rory bit his lip to control his raging temper. Hausser didn't seem the least bit concerned about Paul Michaels's location.

"He'll show up at the purchase," Hausser said over the feed. "That's all that matters."

Rory took the earpiece out and threw it on the floorboard. That was enough. He wasn't going to "sit tight." Not anymore. Time to go in and demand some answers before Hausser completely sabotaged the Henly case.

Rory threw his car into gear and peeled out of the strip mall parking. He ran two red lights then swung his car into the alley behind the furniture store, where he spotted the van pulling away.

His cell chirped.

*Not now,* Rory thought as he pressed Speakerphone and raced his car beside the moving van.

Stroop's voice boomed inside the car. "Just got out of a meeting with both directors and Internal Affairs. Hausser's in this up to his eyeballs. I got suspicious about him having Beaumont. Especially after Fenton found your location and your phone number. Turns out Hausser has been under investigation for a while. He's a leak. He's helping Fenton get his hands on that nanobullet. Anyway, get in there and take over. Maybe you can stop this before it's too late."

"I'm on it, boss. Send me backup. Fast."

Rory found Hausser, behind the wheel of the moving van. He waved for him to pull over. Instead, Hausser accelerated. Rory hit the gas hard, too, and swerved his car into the side of the van. Hausser wasn't going anywhere. His days of feeding information to Anderson Fenton were over.

Rory's Cadillac wasn't much of a match for the large van, but another crash into its side sent it into a stop sign. Rory hopped out, pulled his gun and ran behind the vehicles.

Hausser shifted into Reverse. Rory jumped on the bumper and gripped the overhead storage rack to secure his position. Tucking his gun into his belt, he swung open the back doors.

The van jolted forward again, circling for the other end of the alley. Hausser wouldn't get far. Rory could hear his backup approaching. He swung himself into the rear of the van.

DEA Agent Reams moved toward him, her gun aimed at his chest. "Hausser said you'd do something like this."

"Sorry, Reams." Rory put his hands up and let her get close. Then he disarmed her with a quick movement, pushing her down. Rory aimed his gun at the driver. "Hands up, Hausser."

Hausser stopped the van and slowly turned in his chair to face Rory. His hands hovered just over his thighs.

"On your head!" Rory yelled.

"Drop your gun, Farrell." Agent Reams was behind him now. Rory heard the click of a weapon. She'd grabbed another piece from the well-stocked van.

Hausser laughed.

"He's an informant, Reams," Rory said over his shoulder. "He doesn't care a thing about your drug bust. Isn't that right, Hausser?"

Reams didn't budge. She held the gun steady at Rory's back. He kept his Glock aimed at Hausser's head. Sirens sounded in the distance.

"If you don't believe me, then let's just stay as we are until that backup gets here." Rory glanced behind him to see if Reams agreed. Hausser was on him in an instant.

He shoved Rory and Reams out of the back of the van. Rory grabbed Hausser and pulled him along with them. They fell in a pile to the gravel road and fought for position. A quick struggle for Rory's weapon resulted in Hausser getting flipped to his backside. Reams kicked the weapon out of their reach and held her gun on both men.

"Freeze," she ordered.

The local squad units pulled around the corner and all was sorted out quickly. Rory began thinking about how they could apprehend Michaels. He also wanted to check on Tabitha. Not necessarily in that order.

"Bring him in," Rory instructed the local authorities. He turned to Reams. "Sorry about your drug case. Maybe you could help me out?"

"Would it include ruining him?" Her short blond hair shook as she shot a look of disgust at Hausser.

Rory chuckled. "Most definitely."

"Then count me in," she said, dusting the dirt off her pants.

Rory and Reams headed to Max's office, where Rory hoped to devise a new search plan for Michaels. Sutton, looking embarrassed and defeated, had returned from his unsuccessful tail. Rory hoped he would recover from his mistake enough to be of use.

"Sir, please," the woman at the front desk called after him. Not the receptionist, but one of the assistants that he'd met yesterday.

Rory stopped and showed his badge. "Agent Farrell. We met yesterday. I'm looking for—"

"Yes, you have a phone call," she interrupted. "Would you like to take it here?"

Rory looked around the busy reception. "No. In Dr. Beaumont's office."

She pressed a button and sent the call through. Rory jogged to the back office and picked up the phone.

"Agent Farrell, this is Lieutenant Dillon. I…uh…I tried that number you gave me and couldn't—"

"What is it, Dillon?"

"Miss Beaumont is missing."

# TWENTY-TWO

With Paul's gun pressed into her ribs, Tabitha drove his red Jeep into the country. "What are you doing, Paul?"

"You'll find out soon enough." He jabbed the gun harder into her side.

Tabitha's hands trembled on the wheel. Her right leg shook uncontrollably over the gas pedal.

*Do something. Crash into another car. Get pulled over for speeding.* Isn't that what she'd been told to do to save herself in this sort of situation? Too bad, no other cars seemed to be on the road. Anyway, with a loaded gun cocked at her waist, crashing could mean a bullet in her side. It might have worked earlier when they were in town, but she'd thought Lieutenant Dillon and his partner would be right behind them.

That hadn't happened. Still, Dillon would figure out quickly that she was missing. Then he would call Rory. Rory would find her. Or was that too much to hope for, that he could rescue her three times in the same week? She prayed for it all the same.

She and Paul had been driving for twenty minutes, farther and farther into the rural county west of Richmond. Paul hadn't spoken until now, but he'd checked his watch several times. Tabitha wondered if asking him some questions might distract him, buy her some time or even foil his agenda.

"What do you need me for? Does this have to do with the drugs at the office?" she asked.

"Be quiet, would ya?" Paul growled. "Pull over here."

He indicated a closed-down gas station to the right of the single-lane road. Again, she thought of crashing the car. Why not drive it right into the abandoned station? The Jeep would have air bags.

She took in a deep breath and pressed her leg to the floor, but her quaking foot slipped from the pedal. By the time she'd replaced it, Paul had grabbed the wheel and directed them toward an old-fashioned pay phone to the left of the small parking lot.

"And I thought you were the smart one in the family," he remarked. "If you want to stay alive, I suggest you do what I say. You almost blew us up."

Tabitha looked back and now noticed the large cabinet of rusted propane tanks in front of the old building. *Thanks for letting my foot slip, Lord.*

"That's enough driving for you," Paul mumbled.

Following orders, Tabitha placed the car in Park and cut the engine. Paul tied her wrists together and pushed her out of the car. Without arms to balance, she fell to the concrete ground, knocking the left side of her head, which added another cut to go along with her collection. She could hardly detect the increased ache. The pounding had long been beyond the threshold of tolerance.

She scanned the surrounding farmland. Open fields lay in every direction, nowhere to run for cover. Paul waited for her to crawl to her feet. Then he pushed her to the phone and dialed a number.

"I got what you want," he said. "Come to Aunt Helen's. One hour."

After the call, Paul pushed her back into the car, this time on the passenger side, where he cinched her legs at the knees and ankles with wire that cut into her flesh. She couldn't budge.

Another twenty minutes into the country and nothing but rolling hills of dense woods surrounded them. Paul turned up a hidden gravel path. It wound through the forest for another half mile then dead-ended in a grassy clearing in front of a small clapboard-style rancher. The house needed major repairs. Tabitha noticed hanging gutters, missing shingles and a broken window.

Aunt Helen's? She doubted that even a federal agent could find this place.

Fighting off her discouragement, Tabitha struggled to think of a way to distract Paul. If he untied her legs, maybe she could run into the thick woods and hide. Of course, first he would have to take that stupid gun out of her side. But he might. She had hope. She just had to wait for the right moment.

Tabitha prayed for that moment.

*God, You are in control. Not Paul Michaels.*

Rory paced Max's office and pulled on what little bit of hair he had. If he'd thought it would do any good, he would have hopped in a car and started searching. Hausser was cuffed and sitting in the next room with two police officers watching, but he wouldn't talk.

The only thing they had to go on was the fact that Dillon's partner had seen a red Jeep Commander drive by the Beaumonts' house about ten minutes before Tabitha went missing. No one believed that was a coincidence. Michaels had taken her. There was an APB out for his vehicle. A local unit had been sent to his home. Reams and Sutton were working with the FBI lab to get a location on Michaels's cell. Rory had little hope of it being that simple. Michaels was too smart to leave his cell phone on or go to his own house.

"Why would Paul want my sister?" Max asked.

Rory stopped to look at Tabitha's brother. He was a complete wreck. He'd sent everyone in the office home. Then he'd sat behind his desk with his elbows on his knees and his head folded down in his hands, blaming himself for Tabitha's kidnapping.

Rory continued his path back and forth in front of Max's desk. "Something to do with Henly's files. Michaels knew about your offer from Henly. He cashed in on it, probably by pretending to represent you. I think he has the USB storage device. Maybe he stole it or blackmailed Henly for it. But I have no idea why he needs Tabitha."

Reams knocked at the door. Rory stopped his pacing again.

"No luck with the GPS," she reported. "No one at Michaels's home, either. And no sign of the Jeep."

"Search Michaels's office. His desk. His computer. See if there's anything that might give us a clue as to where he's gone. If he's trading with Fenton today, then it's either going to be some place very public or just the opposite. He'd have to have taken Tabitha by force, which puts my vote on the latter. I'll question Hausser again. I doubt he knows a location but he might be able to give us a time frame."

Reams nodded but didn't turn away. "I apologize for pulling a gun on you," she said. "Hausser came in this week saying he'd had similar cases in Charlotte. He had evidence that they were linked. I thought he knew—"

Rory patted her on the back. "Hey, Hausser has a lot of clout and he used to be a good agent. This isn't your fault, Reams."

Rory walked into the small break room where the two officers guarded Hausser. He dismissed the guards, closed the door and sat opposite the man.

"You're wrong about me," Hausser declared. "I was drawing Fenton in. I was going to get him by letting him trust me."

"Internal Affairs has a huge file on you with all kinds of evidence to support the contrary. If you're so innocent, then prove it. Help us now. Prove you're on the right side."

"I'll wait for my lawyer."

"Then it will be too late," Rory insisted. "You owe me, Hausser."

Hausser bent his head down and scratched it with his cuffed hands.

"What happened to you? Should I have left you in that burning van all those years ago?" Rory waited a few more minutes then he slapped the break table. The sharp sound echoed through the small room. "This is a waste of my time. You're a waste of my time." He stood and headed for the door.

"Wait," Hausser said. "I don't have a way to contact Fenton—he calls me—but he trusts me. Enough to tell me he'd be out of the States by four o'clock today."

Rory stopped before the door and dropped his head. That meant Fenton planned to have Henly's files before four. He checked his watch. They had very little time to stop this transaction. They needed a location. "Where, Hausser? You can't really want that technology to go to terrorists."

Hausser wiggled in his chair. "I don't have a location but Fenton asked me to keep some roads clear in Goochland County."

Rory stared hard at Hausser, wondering if he was lying again or if in his moment of disgrace, he'd decided to do something decent.

Hausser shrugged. "It's all I've got."

Rory clenched his teeth and hustled back to Max's office. "Goochland County. What's in Goochland County?"

*Oh, Lord, please. Please let this lead us to Tabitha.*


Tabitha wished her hand could reach her nose. Aunt Helen's tiny shotgun house harbored a terrible odor. But she couldn't move. After transporting her inside, Paul had bound her wrists and ankles to a chair and secured the chair to a built-in cabinet in the kitchen. She wasn't going anywhere without a saw or a pair of wire cutters.

Now Paul had set up some sort of lab on the counter. From a small tool kit, he grabbed a pair of dental pliers then turned to her. A snarl rolled over his thin lips. Tabitha closed her eyes, wishing she were anywhere but there.

"Time to take out that temporary I made for you," Paul said.

"Max made my temporary," Tabitha retorted.

"Wrong. I traded out the one he made. Now, open up." Paul's thumb and index finger pressed against her cheeks and forced her mouth open. He reached into her mouth and secured the pliers around the temporary crown that Max had put in three weeks ago after her root canal. Paul worked and worked at the tooth until he broke the strong seal of the temporary cement and removed it from her mouth.

"Ouch." The metallic taste of blood coated her tongue. Reluctantly, she swallowed it down.

Paul held up the crown to the light.

"Why did you do that?" she asked. "Just to be mean?"

"You'll see."

He took what looked like a tiny hammer and smashed away the temporary crown. After blowing away the debris, he lifted a tiny chip of metal into the air with a pair of tweezers.

"Ah. Here it is. Perfectly intact." He waved the piece at her proudly. "This is what makes Henly's storage device come to life."

Tabitha's eyes went wide. "*You* had Roger's files?"

"Yep. And so did you."

"What are you talking about?"

Paul laughed, as if the whole thing was a joke. "Roger was so upset when Max didn't want in on his generous offer. I mean, really, how could your brother be so heartless after the guy threw him such a killer bachelor party?"

"So, you stepped in and cheered him up? How nice of you. You got him killed, Paul."

"No. *You* got him killed. You were supposed to have that temporary replaced when the real crown came in. But you decided to run a triathlon instead."

"Why did you stick that chip in my temporary crown? What a crazy idea."

Paul's eyes looked wild. "It's a genius idea. You were my insurance plan."

"You're insane."

"Not at all," Paul continued. "Roger didn't trust me at first. He thought if Max had really changed his mind about the deal then *Max* would have come to him."

"Roger was right," Tabitha mumbled.

"Yeah, well, I told him Max was just being cautious, using me as a go-between. He fell for that hook, line and sinker. But later, I realized I wasn't going to get my cut. So I made sure Roger couldn't get the files without me."

"How is selling…" Tabitha didn't finish her question. She no longer cared to hear how Roger and Paul had plotted to sell government secrets. She just wanted out of there. "Now that you got what you need from me, how about letting me go?"

"What? So you can walk out of here and tell everyone where I am? I don't think so." Paul resumed work. He pulled a small metal and plastic device from a leather case.

Was that the storage drive Rory had spoken of? She couldn't tell. It looked mangled. Paul placed it into some sort of vise and slipped on a pair of latex gloves.

"You have to put that back together? What if it doesn't work?" Tabitha asked.

"It'll work. And if it doesn't, I'll let *you* deliver it to Mr. Fenton."

"If you're so handy with that high-tech stuff, why didn't you just copy the files and sell them yourself?"

Paul looked at her and rolled his eyes. "Roger was stupid, but he wasn't that stupid. He had a double encryption on the device. I couldn't copy it." He turned to her. "But the software doesn't keep the device from running or keep me from taking the drive apart. So when I saw you were coming in for a crown, I took out this key chip and hid it in your temporary. I might not have been able to break the code but this was enough insurance to get what I wanted."

"And what was that?"

"Two million. But now that Roger is…let us say…out of

the picture, I'll be getting a whole lot more." He took a moment to study her expression. "You should have brushed more often, Tabitha."

When he finished laughing at his own bad joke, he went back to work. "So how does it feel knowing you had the important piece all along? I'll bet your agent boyfriend never thought of that, huh?"

*Actually, he did,* Tabitha thought to herself. She couldn't believe it. Rory had been right all along. She'd had Henly's technology and didn't even know it. She dropped her head, ashamed she'd ever worried about putting her trust in him.

Paul turned to her and smiled. "See? It's all about staying a step ahead of everyone. It's easy to do when you consider that most people are stupid."

"Who's stupid? Not me, I hope?" A husky male voice sounded from behind her.

Tabitha turned her head. In the doorway stood a large man holding a pistol. He shuffled his way into the room, filling the small place with his presence. He was muscled, dark-skinned and covered in tattoos. His clothing, however, was top-of-the-line brand-name menswear. The aftershave he wore had a clean, musky scent which was a welcomed change to the damp, nasty odors that filled Aunt Helen's.

Paul jumped at the interruption, almost dropping the metal piece. From the look on his face, Tabitha guessed he had been expecting someone else.

"Frank. Good to see you," Paul said. He tried to keep his voice calm but Tabitha could hear the fear in him.

"Just get my stash," Frank ordered. He sidled over to her. "You're a pretty thing. What are you doing with this loser?"

Tabitha clenched her teeth. "I'm *not* with Paul."

"Interesting." Frank looked at her hands and feet bound to the chair, then back to Paul, who stood motionless. Frank scowled. "Get the stash already."

Frank stepped closer to Paul, positioning his gun at the dentist's head. He cocked the weapon.

Paul hustled over to a large pantry. Inside were shelves and shelves filled with generic, white medicine bottles. Paul loaded half of them into a large cardboard box, put it on the floor and kicked it over to the man with the gun.

"There you go. Paid in full. Now get out of here. I'm working on something." Paul's voice sounded higher than normal and sweat poured from his brow.

Frank opened the back door and knocked the box outside, his gun on Paul. He took a quick step at the dentist. Paul jumped back and whimpered.

Frank laughed. "You're too stupid to waste a bullet on, but here's the thing. Word on the street is that the DEA is onto you. So, no more contact with me. Understand?"

If it was possible, Paul looked even more nervous. "No, man. You got some bad info."

Frank stepped closer to Paul. "Okay then. Listen up. Contact me again and you won't live. *Now* do you understand? And here's something to help you remember."

Frank landed a right hook on Paul's left cheek. Paul flopped to the ground, hitting his head on the kitchen table as he fell. He was out cold, but not dead. Tabitha could still see his chest rise and fall with his breathing.

Frank turned to her with a mischievous grin. "If only I had the time." He grazed his fingers down the length of her face then leaned over her.

Tabitha stiffened.

"He's got you tied up good." He hung his gun in his belt and flipped open a switchblade. Then the man reached down behind her. Tabitha felt the knife pull at one of the wires around her wrist. He worked and worked the knife until one wire popped. "That will get you started. Good luck."

He stepped back, put away the knife and left.

Tabitha breathed deeply for the first time since Paul had taken her from her brother's. She began working her wrists against the thickly wound wires that bound her. Maybe somehow she could loosen them and get out of there before Paul came to.

# TWENTY-THREE

"Goochland County." Max stood from behind his desk, his face hopeful. "Yeah, yeah. Paul had an old aunt or uncle that lived there."

"You got a name?" Rory asked, the hope starting to build in him.

"Uh…Myers. No. Mason. No. Mayfield… Oh, man, it starts with an *M*." Max shook his head back and forth.

"Come on. This is your sister," Rory prompted. "Think."

"Matheson. Helen Matheson. She died a few years ago and left the place to Paul. She used to be a patient. We might still have a file. Elise never throws anything away." Max ran out of the office toward the front of the building.

Rory called Sutton and Reams inside. "We have a possible location. Goochland County. Home of Helen Matheson."

Sutton nodded. "Yes. I saw that name on a magazine in Michaels's office. I'll get it." He turned to the other office.

Max flew back into the room with a green file folder. "2200 Old Forest Way. I've been there. It's in the country about thirty minutes from here."

Rory took a deep breath, his heart starting to beat steadily again. "Describe it."

"Paul had asked me to help him move some of the furniture out after his aunt died. It's probably two hundred acres of woods with a single-floor home right in the middle. Simple. No basement. No garage. Very isolated."

"Sounds like a good prospect." Rory turned to Reams. "Is the van equipped?"

She nodded. "You banged it up a little, but it'll run."

"Then let's go. We'll talk strategy on the way," Rory said.

Max followed them out of the building.

"You can't come," Rory stated flatly.

"I'm coming," Max declared and climbed into the van.

Paul sat up and rubbed his head where it had crashed into the table. Tabitha sat perfectly still so he couldn't see the loose wires around her wrists.

She didn't know how long he'd been out. Five minutes or so. Not long enough for her to work her hands free. But she had loosened them. Soon, she would be able to slip her hands through completely.

Paul went to work immediately on the device. His hands shook as he cleaned the piece he'd taken from her tooth, but he kept working steadily. Next, he wedged the chip into the open device with tweezers. Then he welded the structure with the tiniest soldering torch she'd ever seen. When it cooled, he snapped a cover over the exposed portion and removed it from the vise grips.

Tabitha couldn't believe it. It looked like any USB storage drive for sale at a local office supply store.

"Let's make sure this baby still works." Paul sat at the dirty kitchen table and plugged the new drive into a large laptop. His lips curved in an evil twist as the file menu lit up on the screen. He checked a few things then unplugged the device and the computer. "Perfect. Now, we wait."

"So, you're the one dealing the Vicodin, too?"

"I won't need to do that anymore." He sat back in his chair. "Although it was a pretty good gig until the DEA started checking on foreign prescription drug sales. I've spent the past three months covering my tracks. When this little house blows up, so will anything linking me to that."

"The house is going to blow up?" Tabitha repeated. Her heart leaped into her throat. She started working her wrists again. She didn't care if Paul did see her.

Rory prayed that Aunt Helen's home in Goochland County was the location Paul had chosen. If nothing else he just wanted to find Tabitha there. Unharmed. Just like he'd left her. If they found Henly's storage drive and Michaels or Fenton or DeWitt there, too, then that would be icing on the cake. But all he really wanted was to see Tabitha again. He wished he'd never left her.

On the way, he and Sutton studied layouts of the forest and the roads surrounding the old country house—anything they could get their hands on via the van satellite and GPS systems.

Rory had to hand it to Paul. It was a well-chosen location. There was only one private road that gave access in or out of the property. Rory noted a small creek that ran from the highway to the house. That was helpful. It would give them a path to follow off the road, under the cover of the dense forest surrounding the home.

In case Fenton and DeWitt were there making a deal, Rory decided it would be best if they approached on foot. Reams would station the van as close as possible without remaining visible to the main road. Rory and Agent Sutton had to get in fast and assess the situation. Max was to stay inside the van. Rory hoped he would.

Stroop had called in a SWAT team, but it could take them up to forty minutes to come by land. Just in case, a small force arriving in a helicopter would be there in less than ten.

Rory faced Sutton as the young man checked and rechecked his weapon. "Is this your first op?"

He nodded. "I just finished the academy last month."

"Then your skills should be sharp."

"I wasn't in the service first like you were," he added.

Rory grinned. "We rescue first. Attain the files second. Apprehend third. Can you remember that?"

The man nodded.

"Then let's go." Rory spotted the creek he'd landmarked on the map and turned to Reams. "I want off here."

The van stopped quickly. He and Agent Sutton descended. They dashed into the cover of the thick forest and headed due north following the creek. By Rory's estimation, they would reach the house in less than five minutes.

Agent Sutton kept close. He was green, but seemed in good condition. He was certainly alert and probably eager to redeem himself after losing Michaels. His presence helped Rory focus on the task at hand and not on the dangers that Tabitha could be in. For that he was thankful.

His own adrenaline kicked in hard as he and Sutton scrambled toward the house. Would Michaels be there? DeWitt? Fenton? No one?

*Oh, God, please let her be there. Please. Alive and well.*

Rory gritted his teeth. Losing Tabitha was not an option. And before this day was over, he planned to tell her that.

Rory spotted the house at eleven o'clock about one hundred yards out. He checked over his shoulder to find Sutton had slowed a bit but was just a few yards back. He motioned for Sutton to stay put while he moved in closer. He pressed his earpiece. "One red Jeep Commander outside. No other vehicle. Checking perimeter."

Paul had started to pace the house from front to back. "Something's wrong. It's taking too long."

Each time he left the kitchen, Tabitha worked her hands against the wires. She continued to pray that Rory would find her, although she knew it was impossible.

*No. Not impossible,* she corrected herself. *Improbable. With God all things are possible....*

And God was in control. She'd never forget the promise

she'd made that morning. She'd do whatever she could to keep Him in control. Acknowledging that, Tabitha felt more alive than she had in years. She was ready—ready to heal, ready to marry, ready to have children and grow old with someone—whatever God had in mind. For the first time in two years, Tabitha wanted to live...not just exist.

Her left hand, red and raw, popped free from the wires and then her right. With Paul hovering in the next room, she bent over to undo the restraints around her ankles.

The drapes were open. Plenty of light shone in. Michaels's car was parked to the side. But it looked empty. Nothing seemed to move inside the house.

Rory didn't like it. Had they taken too long? Already missed Michaels? He didn't know. But he was suffering from the worst case of operation jitters in his life.

"There are fresh tracks from another vehicle," Rory said over his wire. "May have changed cars. House looks empty. I'm going in."

Turning to Sutton, he motioned for the rookie to move closer while he took a position at the other end of the house. Rory moved fast and low, studying the doors and windows as he moved. The back door looked wired, booby-trapped maybe.

As he moved to the opposite side of the house, he found the front door was similarly armed. "Two doors. They look hot," he announced.

Reams's voice sounded in his ear. "Your bird is in position. And you've got company. A black SUV. The plates aren't in the system."

DeWitt. Or Fenton. Maybe even both. Rory's gut tightened. "Let it come. Then block the driveway at the road. Send in four men from the chopper on foot."

Two minutes later the black SUV rolled across the gravel that led to the small house. It parked at the front door and two men stepped out of the passenger side—Victor DeWitt and

Anderson Fenton. Including a driver, that made three. He and Sutton were outnumbered without even considering who else could be inside. They'd have to stay put and wait for backup. Two more minutes.

The front door opened. Michaels appeared and waved Fenton inside. But Fenton raised a gun. Michaels disappeared behind the door. Fenton fired and Sutton broke out of his post, weapon raised.

*Too soon, Sutton.* Backup was still a good minute out. Fool kid was going to get himself killed.

Rory took a deep breath and ran in. He went low, toward the front of the vehicle, but it was too late. DeWitt spotted Sutton and took a shot. Sutton hit the ground, grabbing his shoulder and trying to roll to his side.

"Stay down, Sutton," Rory ordered, relieved the kid was still moving. "Move in, Reams."

Rory pulled his gun on Fenton, but he and DeWitt had already climbed back into the SUV. O'Conner was at the wheel. He accelerated, racing the vehicle at Rory.

Rory dived and rolled. DeWitt fired two shots at him from the back window. One bullet grazed the skin on his hip. A familiar burn radiated through his side, but he stood, blocking the pain from his thoughts, and raised his Glock. The SUV turned to exit down the gravel drive. They wouldn't get far with Reams blocking them. Still, he fired two shots at the vehicle's tires, hitting one of them. That would slow them down. "Coming your way, Reams. Where's that 'copter?"

As soon as he'd said it, Rory heard the whir of chopper blades. More than one of them. Rory grinned. Stroop was a smart man.

Rory turned back to the house. Sutton lay still on the ground. At the edge of the woods, Rory spotted his four SWAT boys moving in. He sent one of them to Sutton, one to him and the other two to cover the back.

A well-equipped SWAT member approached.

"I think there's a woman inside," Rory informed him. "But the house looks wired."

The SWAT officer moved to the door and looked over the setup. Rory stayed low under the window. He had no idea if Michaels was still inside, if he was armed, if he'd been injured, if he had Tabitha…

Sutton sat up with the help of the other man. DeWitt had shot him in the shoulder.

"Michaels went…" Sutton spoke with labored breaths over his wire. "Out the back…alone."

Michaels would have a good head start but if those SWAT guys were any good, they'd catch him before he reached the road.

"Tabitha?" Rory yelled.

"In here." Her voice sounded faint. "I'm tied up."

"Sit tight. I'm coming," he said and looked down at the man working on the wires. "What's the verdict?"

"It's wired for something. But there's no trigger here," he said.

"That's good enough." Rory plowed through the door. The sickening sweet smell of gasoline hit his nostrils as soon as he entered. An accelerant. The house was wired to burn.

"Please be you, Rory." Tabitha's voice came from a nearby room.

He found her in the kitchen. Her feet were tied to a heavy chair that was well fixed to the cabinetry, but her hands were free. She was bent over, working her fingers as fast as she could on the restraints around her ankles and she was crying.

"It's me." He pulled her face up and kissed her hard.

"I didn't cry until I heard you," she said.

"Cry all you want, baby. It's the best sound I've ever heard." His heart raced as he crouched to untie the mass of wires that bound her legs to the chair. "And hold still. I don't have time to be gentle."

"Paul ran out the back. He has Henly's files."

"There are men on him. They'll catch him," he stated, concentrating on the twisted wire.

"He said he's going to blow up the house. He said it's hiding all the evidence."

Her feet now freed, Rory locked eyes with her. "I think you're right."

A loud click sounded as he reached for her. Rory grabbed Tabitha at the waist, pulled her to his shoulder and ran from the kitchen as the small room became engulfed with wicked flames. Intense heat at his back, a new blaze in the front, Rory knew he wouldn't make it to either door.

"Hold tight," he said to Tabitha, tucking her head into his neck. Then he dived through the dining-room window, twisting his figure to take the brunt of the fall as they hit the ground. He rolled and scrambled, holding Tabitha tight against his chest. He gained just ten yards before the entire house exploded.

Rory pushed her face down and covered her body with his own.

# TWENTY-FOUR

"Come home with us," Karin whispered to Tabitha from the edge of the ICU curtain enclosing Rory's bed.

"She's right, Tabs. The doctor will call us when he wakes up." Max nodded in agreement with his wife.

*If* he wakes up…

Tabitha swallowed hard. She felt her brother's warm hand on her shoulder but didn't respond. Ever since the nurses had allowed her into the intensive care unit—solely due to the fact that Karin's family had built the facility—she hadn't moved from Rory's side. The nurses said that it was crucial he wake soon. She would wait. She owed him that. She owed him her life.

He'd been badly hurt in the explosion. The flaming debris had struck him in several places. When she'd rolled out from under his protection at the scene, she'd never seen so much blood. Her brother had had to drag her away from his unresponsive body to allow the medical team to come in. Now, hours later, she still waited for a response.

Max gave her shoulder another squeeze. "He'll be in so much pain. You don't want to see him like that. Come back in the morning. We need to talk."

With a tired smile, Tabitha turned to her family and retreated with them from the small ICU space to the nurses' station.

"I told him about Roger," Karin explained.

Tabitha closed her eyes and let out a deep sigh. "I'd hoped you would. Thank you." Her sister-in-law would never know how grateful she was not to have to tell her brother that story. "I'm glad you both know. I should have told you two years ago. I'm sorry that I didn't."

"You're sorry? I'm sorry. I pushed you to go out with him. I thought…" He enveloped her in his arms. "I thought I knew him. I'm so angry I swear it's a good thing he's not around. I'd—"

Tabitha shook her head. "Let it go, Max. For me. Please. What Roger did was no more your fault than my own."

Her brother punched his fist into his open hand. "Give me some time. Right now, I have to be mad."

Tabitha smiled weakly. "I understand that more than you know. Why don't you two go home? We'll talk later."

"You're really not coming?" Karin said with concern. "Truly, you need to rest. You must be exhausted."

She shook her head. "I can't."

Max gave his sister a kiss on the forehead. "Farrell's a good man. He was as upset as I was when Paul had you. Tried to pull that little bit of hair he's got right out of his head. Wore my office carpet out pacing back and forth."

Tabitha grinned. "Now it's my turn to worry."

"I heard the burns were bad," Karin commented. "My dad called in a specialist from Duke Medical, a friend of his. Agent Farrell is a hero. He'll be getting the VIP treatment while he's here."

"Thank you, Karin." The burns *were* bad. Third degree on his shoulder and thigh. But it was the head injury that posed the most danger. "He needs to wake up soon and if he's in pain that's good. That means everything's working the way it should. Until then we have to worry about a coma, paralysis, memory loss." Tabitha clasped her hands together to keep them from shaking.

"He's tough. He'll be fine." Max's way of saying he'd pray. "Call us."

Karin held her hand for a minute. Then the couple turned away and left the ICU.

Tabitha slid back behind the curtain. The fact that Rory's large body didn't fit on the bed made her smile. Turned on his side so as not to lie directly on the burns, his bare feet hung exposed over the end of the bed. She rubbed them with her hands, wondering if he could even feel her fingers. If he ever would feel them. If he would even remember her. The chances for paralysis were great. The possibility of recent memory loss even greater.

For now, his face looked peaceful. Besides the tubes from the IV fluids, he appeared to be enjoying a nap. The occasional tremor and spasms in his eyelids reminded her that he was far from resting. Rory was fighting to live.

The hours passed slowly. His body became more restless and his face less peaceful. That ruled out paralysis and they moved him to Recovery. Tabitha followed.

In Recovery, she pulled a chair close to his head. She sat and held his hand, continuing to pray and whisper to him. Although a few times in her own exhaustion, her head fell forward in a light doze.

Awakened from her catnap, she found his face twisted in pain as he moaned. She hated his agony but rejoiced in it all the same.

He finally cried out and two nurses hustled into the room. They tried to whisk her away as they ran tests and worked on him. When she pulled away, he held tight to her hand.

"Stay," he whispered. His body stiffened from the effort and he struggled to breathe.

"If you promise to be good and not scare me anymore." She caught his deep blue eyes as they flickered open. Her fingers closed around his hand. She was so thankful he remembered her.

"You okay?" he asked then groaned in agony as one of the nurses poked at him.

"I'm perfect," she answered.

At her response, his face relaxed. His eyes closed and his body went still. He was drifting back to unconsciousness. His monitors began to alarm. The nurses pressed buttons and ordered the doctor in.

"No!" Tabitha cried. She couldn't lose him now. She squeezed his hand but it had gone limp. "No. Wake up. Stay with me." *I love you.*

"You'll have to leave. We need room to work," one nurse said with no emotion.

"Please," Tabitha pleaded, but the nurse was already guiding her from the room. Tabitha felt powerless. She didn't want to leave. What if he'd gone into a coma? She hadn't even said thank you.

*Lord, please bring him back.*

After two long hours, a doctor found her in the waiting room.

"Mr. Farrell is in severe pain. He's very weak from blood loss and the concussion. We've got him on a lot of morphine for the burns. But his condition is temporary. He's going to be fine. The CT showed that there's no permanent brain damage."

Tabitha closed her eyes and pressed her hands to her cheeks. *Thank You, Lord.* A massive weight had been lifted from her shoulders. "And he's okay? He's awake?"

"Not a thing wrong with him except for a headache and the burns, which will heal in a few weeks. He'll be good as new."

"Thank you," Tabitha said, close to weeping from fatigue and joy. *Thank You, Lord.*

"He's asking for you," the doctor relayed.

"May I see him?"

He nodded. "But don't push him too hard and don't expect him to make a lot of sense."

Tabitha grinned and eagerly headed to his room.

"When's the wedding?" the doctor called after her.

She lifted her eyebrows as she turned back. "He told you that we're engaged?"

The doctor shrugged. "Something to that effect."

Tabitha smiled. The morphine had already confused him. Still, she considered for a moment how it might feel to be engaged to Rory Farrell. He was so strong, so intense, a little pushy. Okay, very pushy. He was a bull. Maybe she would like having a bull in her life. In fact, the idea filled her heart with joy.

"We're not engaged," she answered with a blush. "Yet." Then she turned and headed to his room.

"You stayed here the whole time?" he whispered. "Thank you."

Tabitha lifted her head from the back of the chair where she'd fallen asleep waiting for him to wake up again. She smiled. Rory felt pleasure at the mere sight of it. He loved that smile. He loved that woman.

She still wore the ensemble she'd borrowed from the FBI safe house. It was a little tattered and torn, still too big, and she looked completely adorable.

"Actually, I wasn't here the whole time. You were here for a while all by yourself," she teased. "They brought you by helicopter. I had to come in a car."

"That couldn't be good if I was in a helicopter. What happened?"

Tabitha pushed her chair closer and took his hand. "The house blew up."

He wanted to laugh but his body wouldn't let him. Just to smile was painful. "Don't be cute. Can't take cute right now."

"But I'm always cute."

He wanted so badly to hug her but his body wouldn't do anything he asked. "Yes. Yes, you are. But seriously. After the explosion, what happened? Did Agent Reams get Fenton?"

"Yes. And DeWitt. And O'Conner. Your backup team got Michaels in the woods. Just not in time to keep him from detonating the house."

"He did that by remote?"

She nodded.

"And Henly's files?"

"Safely back at the Office of Naval Research." She patted his hand. "You know Paul was behind the drugs, too. Your boss has him. Apparently, he's naming everyone he can, trying to save himself. And you were right. He hid a chip in that temporary crown Max put on my tooth three weeks ago. It made the storage drive work. I had it all along and didn't know it, just like you said."

"I didn't really want to be right about that. Did he pull off your cap?"

"Yep."

"So, you have a hole in your mouth?" he asked with a frown.

"You have third-degree burns and you're worried about a hole in my mouth?" She tilted her head. "Well, don't worry. Max is going to put the porcelain crown in later. That is, once I see that you don't fall asleep on me."

"I promise to be good," he whispered. "So, Max and the other agents are okay? Sutton?"

"Sutton got shot. But he's fine. Everyone's fine." She paused and looked deeply into his eyes. "My parents are on their way from England. They'll stay as long as needed. They wouldn't believe that we were okay. Said they had to see for themselves."

"That's nice," he murmured.

"Yes…I'm glad they're coming…I need to talk to them and they want to meet you, of course. I mean…I want them to meet you. Would you?"

He squeezed her hand. He would have smiled if he could have. Meeting her parents? That had to mean something.

"Oh, and your cousin Terri is on her way with Gram and Mr. Watson. They'll stay with my parents until you're released. They postponed the wedding."

"You called them?" he guessed.

She nodded.

"Thank you for that. How long will I be here?"

"A week at the very least. You know, you've gotten lots of gifts. Even one from the Secretary of Defense. The nurses said between your fed friends and the people of Hendersonville, you have more balloons and flowers than anyone in Recovery history. Of course, I think they're exaggerating because they're all in love with you."

"Hadn't noticed." He tried to lace his fingers through hers, but his brain was foggy with pain. His eyes kept closing, telling him to sleep. But he didn't want to leave this moment.

"Where are all these gifts?" he asked.

"Karin had them sent to a private room, which I understand is not an easy thing to get in this place. They'll move you there in a few hours."

"Tell her thank you."

"Tell her yourself. She's coming for a visit and an inspection to make sure you're getting the royal treatment."

This time when he looked up at her, he saw the terrible fatigue in her face. She needed rest. As did he. He forced his brain to clear enough to speak again. "Go home, Tabitha. You look worn-out."

"Ha. Even incapacitated you're a bull."

"I'm a what?"

"You're a bull."

Her soft brown eyes met his. He loved the way they twinkled. He didn't want to lose this woman. At the same time, he didn't want to break his own heart. He had to know now if there was any hope for him.

"Think you could learn to love a bull?"

"I think I want to give it a try." She leaned over and kissed him on the forehead.

The shock of her words revived him. He felt his heart racing with joy. "Tabitha?"

"Yes, Bull."

"Will you…will you go on a date with me when I get out of here?"

She laughed. "How about we start with that thank-you dinner I owe you?"

"Deal. Now, go to your brother's and get some sleep."

# TWENTY-FIVE

*Three months later*

Just one more mile. Tabitha cruised along Queens Boulevard under its canopy of spindling oaks. The colors of the trees, now at the season's peak, ranged from a brilliant yellow to the deepest red. Autumn, her favorite time of year—the sun still warmed her skin, but the air felt crisp. She filled her lungs in a slow draw then exhaled just as methodically. Her body in complete sync from head to toe.

Just a couple of minutes to the finish.

She and Max had entered the Charlotte Thanksgiving Triathlon together and had been fortunate enough to be placed in the same flight. They'd stayed together during the first two phases, the swimming and biking. But she'd told her brother to go on during the run. His stride was too quick for her and she didn't care about finishing in the top half. She just wanted to finish.

Rory hadn't raced. She knew he'd been torn about leaving her for the weekend, but he'd promised to be with his family. And she saw plenty of Rory. He'd moved to Charlotte to work for the FBI. Hausser had been replaced with a good man and Rory had become his terrorist unit leader. Rory's job truly kept him busy, but they'd still fit a year's worth of dating into a few months. She couldn't have been happier.

Tabitha continued along the city streets she knew so well. She and Rory had jogged this route three mornings a week for the past six weeks for her training. She wished he were here now, enjoying her first finish.

"I like the look on your face," the familiar voice said behind her. "It's a good race. You're doing well. Good time."

In her periphery, she saw Rory running one step behind her. Within seconds he caught her, passed her, turned around and ran backward in front of her.

"Show off." She smiled with the pleasure she always felt at seeing him. His brown wavy hair had grown out, framing his impossibly blue eyes. Gorgeous. Tabitha wouldn't mind looking at him for the rest of her life. "When did you get back?"

"This morning. I couldn't miss your race. I picked up Gram and Mr. Watson and brought them here. They're with Karin at the finish. Max came in a few minutes ago."

Tabitha lifted her eyes to him. "Thanks for coming."

"Oh…and I brought you something." He grinned mischievously.

She nodded. She'd already seen the Gatorade in his hand. "Good call." She reached for the drink but he pulled it back.

"But wait. I have something else in my other hand. You might like it, too. But you only get to pick one."

Tabitha swatted at him with one hand and grabbed the Gatorade from him with the other. Berry-flavored, her favorite. She *really* wanted it. She continued to run as she lifted it to her lips. The cold drink felt like silk sliding down her dry throat. Just a few sips. She knew better than to drink too much. She handed it back. At the finish, she'd happily drink the rest.

"Aren't you curious what you gave up for a sip of sports drink?" he asked.

"Nope."

"Really? Not the least bit curious?"

"No, because you'll give it to me anyway."

He blinked his eyes rapidly as if astonished by her boldness. "You think so?"

"Yes. To keep me happy…" She paused for a few strides, catching her breath. "You'll have to." Tabitha hoped desperately that it was a banana or a PowerBar. Just a taste would be perfect.

"You know me too well," he said. He turned around and jogged beside her. He held out his pinky finger. The end of it held a small gold ring with a diamond solitaire that sparkled in the sun's rays. His face looked as pale as when he'd been in the hospital with a concussion.

Tabitha stopped right there. Right in the middle of the street. Right in the middle of the race. Her mouth open, partly from shock, partly from heavy breathing that she couldn't control. "That's not a PowerBar," she noted.

"No. It's not a PowerBar." Rory searched her face, but shock had prevented her from reacting. "Tabitha, you don't have to take it now. But when you're ready…I would be honored if… Well, I'd like for you to—"

His words pulled her back. Her bull was nervous. Who would have guessed? A warm feeling tingled through her entire being. This was right. This was God's will. Still, she couldn't resist a little taunting. "Spit it out. I've got a race to run here."

He cradled her face in his hands. "Marry me," he said. "And keep moving or you'll cramp."

She held up her hand and let him slide the ring over her finger. She gave him a quick kiss and went back to running. Maybe she sprinted. A sudden boost of energy had filled her body.

"Was that a yes?" he shouted from behind.

She turned her head and grinned. "That was a big yes. Now, come on." She waved him to her. "Run with me."

\* \* \* \* \*

Dear Reader,

I'm so glad you decided to pick up this book. I hope you enjoyed Tabitha and Rory's story. *Protector's Honor* is particularly special to me because it's my first and when I found out that Steeple Hill had decided to buy it, I had just come home from spending nearly six weeks in the hospital with GBS, where God had been my own great Protector.

Many people have asked me where I got this story idea. Believe it or not, I got the idea from a middle school student. A few years ago when I was teaching, I had a student who was obsessed with nanotechnology and through him, I became interested. It also helped that my husband is a dentist.

I love to hear from readers. I hope you'll visit me at my Web site and drop me a note: www.kitwilkinson.com.

May God's blessing be always with you and yours.

*Kit Wilkinson*

## QUESTIONS FOR DISCUSSION

1. At the start of the story, Tabitha Beaumont is only comfortable when she is in control of the world around her. Have you ever tried to force things a certain way or tried to avoid situations because you feared an unknown outcome? Did your efforts protect you?

2. Rory Farrell is angry over his father's painful death. Think of times in your own life when you might have questioned God's sovereignty. How do we reconcile these questions without always understanding the purpose of certain life occurrences?

3. In the opening scene, Rory risks his life to help a stranger in need. This example is extreme; however, every day presents us with opportunities to help our neighbors. Are there any such situations you've passed over recently? Why is this an important manifestation of faith?

4. Paul Michaels and Roger Henly are driven by greed and power. What are the consequences of their obsessions and self-indulgence? Who do you know that has been a victim of someone else's reckless behavior? How has it affected them?

5. Tabitha thinks she's dealt with her rape, but as soon as Rory mentions Roger's name, she falls apart. Have you ever been surprised by a memory or emotion that you thought you'd overcome?

6. One in six women will be sexually assaulted in their lifetime. Seventy-three percent of rape victims know their assailants. (Cited from rain.org.) Healing from such an ex-

perience is difficult and time-consuming; in what ways does Rory help Tabitha heal? How did her own pride get in the way of her healing?

7. Tabitha's rape was clearly not her fault and yet she carried a lot of guilt from the experience. Why? How did this hinder all her other relationships? What are some things that she didn't do that could have helped her through the experience?

8. Max is a good person, but has difficulty reading others and is taken advantage of. Where do you draw the line between a friend and someone using you? Is it always clear, or do you tend to end up on one side or the other? How does that make you feel?

9. Fear is a motivator. Fear of the unknown. Fear of harm. Fear of loss. Fear of failure. In this story, there are many scenes where characters are driven by fear. Cite a few and decide if the outcome of the character's action is positive or negative.

10. The Bible tells us to never fear. If the characters would have acted out of love instead of fear, how would that have changed the story? Which character(s) do(es) act out of love and not fear?

11. Tabitha has to put her trust in someone she hardly knows. Why is this difficult for her even though she feels God's hand in Rory's presence? Do you ever feel resistant to move in directions that God wants you?

12. What's your favorite moment in the story? Why?

Private investigator Wade Sutton plans to hightail it out of Dry Creek long before December 25. The town holds too many *unmerry* memories. Until he's asked to watch over a woman in danger, a woman whose faith changes him forever.

*Turn the page for a sneak preview of*
*SILENT NIGHT IN DRY CREEK*
*by Janet Tronstad.*
*Available in October 2009*
*from Love Inspired ®*

Wade wished he had never come back to Dry Creek. Or, since he had come back, he wished people hadn't been so kind to him. Barbara making that cake for him was putting him off his game. And then Jasmine—usually he didn't have any trouble taking a tough line with a suspect. But then, he'd never been tempted to kiss a suspect before.

He watched Jasmine's back as she walked to the table. She was ramrod straight and angry with him. He knew he'd come on too strong, but it was either that or forgetting everything he knew about law enforcement and refusing to believe she could be responsible for anything.

As a lawman he had to consider all the possibilities, and it was hard to forget that Lonnie had been her partner. She could have sent him a coded message that in some way had helped him escape from prison, or at least given him an incentive to risk everything to get outside.

He wished he knew how to look into the heart of a person so he would know what Jasmine was thinking. Was she as innocent as she looked, or as guilty as she had been the first time she was convicted of a crime? He knew better than most how many ex-cons fell back into theft. He was often the one who took them in the second time around and listened to their sorry excuses.

"I gave you the biggest piece of cake," Barbara said as he sat down at his place at the table.

"Thank you." Wade smiled. It was the cake of his childhood fantasies, and he was going to have to force himself to eat it. All he wanted to do was take Jasmine home and then park his car at the end of the lane to her father's place. Why did she have to be tied up with Lonnie? Why couldn't she be a nice, ordinary woman like Barbara here? Carl never had to worry about arresting *her*.

Wade felt the smoothness of the cake on his tongue and the sweet tang of the raspberry filling. He smiled up at Barbara and thanked her again for the cake. The two kids at the table were smacking their lips and demanding more, just as Wade would be doing if he wasn't so troubled.

Then he looked down the table and saw his dear friend Edith. She wouldn't be happy about him keeping an eye on anyone. It was clear the older woman was very fond of Jasmine. That, of course, was the problem with being a lawman and trying to have friends. He liked things black and white with no shades of gray. He didn't want to have feelings for the suspect.

By doing his job, he was going to upset Jasmine and everyone else in Dry Creek. For the first time since he'd driven into town, he missed the barren feel of his apartment in Idaho Falls. He knew who he was there.

It didn't take long for Wade to leave the Walls' house, with Jasmine walking in front of him. The night was cold. Jasmine wrapped her arms around her body to keep warm and hurried to his car. He was still nursing that leg of his, so he went more slowly than she did. He made it in good time, though, and as he opened the car door for her, she nodded her thanks and slid into the passenger seat.

The first thing Wade did after he got into the car was to move the dial up on the heater. Snowflakes were just starting to fall, but they were scattered enough that he could clear them away with his windshield wipers.

He silently turned his car around and started down the sheriff's lane. The car lights shone on the falling snow, making the flakes look like pinpricks in the darkness.

"You don't think Lonnie would do something to my father, do you?" Jasmine asked. She looked up at him with eyes full of worry. "Lonnie's not very stable. I wouldn't want anyone around here to be hurt by him."

Wade shrugged. "With all you'd inherit if Elmer were out of the picture—"

Jasmine gasped. "I don't care about the money."

"Lonnie might."

That turned her quiet. He didn't want her to worry, though.

"He won't even have the chance to get close to anyone," Wade assured her. "We'll have the feds all over the place by tomorrow. Lonnie has a better chance of breaking in to Fort Knox than he has of sneaking into Dry Creek."

Wade hoped he wasn't lying. He had no idea what the feds would do. And they might have some completely different theories as to why Lonnie had broken out of prison. It might have nothing at all to do with Jasmine or anyone in Dry Creek.

"You'll be safe," Wade said as he opened his door.

He walked around to the passenger door and opened it. Wade stood by the open car door and watched as Jasmine pulled her coat closer to her body. She wasn't making any move to walk toward the house and he wasn't making any move to let her. Finally Wade reached out and touched her cheek. It was soft and a little damp. She must have been crying when she'd been huddled against the door on the drive out here.

"It'll be okay," he whispered to her as he brought his hand down.

"I'm fine," she said.

He nodded with a slight smile. "I know."

Wade had never kissed a suspect, but he would have done it now if he hadn't thought it would make Jasmine cry even more. She was barely hanging on, and he needed to leave her with her dignity.

"I'll be parked at the end of Elmer's lane if you need me,"

Wade said as he stepped back from the door. Snow was falling in earnest now, but in his trunk he had a heavy sleeping bag that he used on stakeouts like this. "I'll come to the door in the morning, before I go over to my grandfather's."

"You can't sleep outside all night. It's freezing out here. I'll leave the kitchen door unlocked in case you need to come inside."

"Don't leave anything unlocked. I'll duck into the barn if I need to."

Jasmine nodded.

Wade watched her walk to the kitchen door and go inside the house. Only then did he head back to the driver's door. He wondered if he'd get any sleep tonight. He was losing his edge. The next thing he knew, he was going to be offering pillows to everyone he arrested and wishing them sweet dreams. When had he turned into a soft touch?

He waited for the light to go out in the kitchen before he started his drive down the lane. He already felt lonely.

* * * * *

*Will Jasmine give Wade reason to*
*call Dry Creek home again?*
*Find out in*
*SILENT NIGHT IN DRY CREEK*
*by Janet Tronstad.*
*Available in October 2009*
*from Love Inspired®*

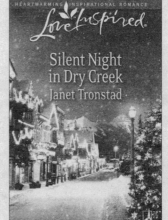

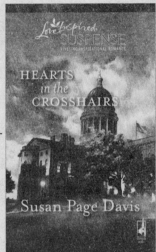

# REQUEST YOUR FREE BOOKS!
## 2 FREE RIVETING INSPIRATIONAL NOVELS
## PLUS 2 FREE MYSTERY GIFTS

**YES!** Please send me 2 FREE Love Inspired® Suspense novels and my 2 FREE mystery gifts (gifts are worth about $10). After receiving them, if I don't wish to receive any more books, I can return the shipping statement marked "cancel". If I don't cancel, I will receive 4 brand-new novels every month and be billed just $4.24 per book in the U.S. or $4.74 per book in Canada. That's a savings of over 20% off the cover price. It's quite a bargain! Shipping and handling is just 50¢ per book.* I understand that accepting the 2 free books and gifts places me under no obligation to buy anything. I can always return a shipment and cancel at any time. Even if I never buy another book, the two free books and gifts are mine to keep forever.

123 IDN EYM2   323 IDN EYNE

| | | |
|---|---|---|
| Name | (PLEASE PRINT) | |
| Address | | Apt. # |
| City | State/Prov. | Zip/Postal Code |

Signature (if under 18, a parent or guardian must sign)

### Mail to Steeple Hill Reader Service:
**IN U.S.A.:** P.O. Box 1867, Buffalo, NY 14240-1867
**IN CANADA:** P.O. Box 609, Fort Erie, Ontario L2A 5X3

Not valid to current subscribers of Love Inspired Suspense books.

**Want to try two free books from another series?**
**Call 1-800-873-8635 or visit www.morefreebooks.com**

\* Terms and prices subject to change without notice. Prices do not include applicable taxes. Sales tax applicable in N.Y. Canadian residents will be charged applicable provincial taxes and GST. Offer not valid in Quebec. This offer is limited to one order per household. All orders subject to approval. Credit or debit balances in a customer's account(s) may be offset by any other outstanding balance owed by or to the customer. Please allow 4 to 6 weeks for delivery. Offer available while quantities last.

**Your Privacy:** Steeple Hill Books is committed to protecting your privacy. Our Privacy Policy is available online at www.SteepleHill.com or upon request from the Reader Service. From time to time we make our lists of customers available to reputable third parties who may have a product or service of interest to you. If you would prefer we not share your name and address, please check here. ☐

LISUS09

# Love Inspired
## HISTORICAL
### INSPIRATIONAL HISTORICAL ROMANCE

After years of caring for others, Nola Burns is ready to live her own dream of running a Nantucket tearoom. And it will take more than charm for dashing entrepreneur Harrison Starbuck to buy her out. All Harry offers is a business proposition. So why should it bother him when Nola starts receiving threatening notes? As the threats escalate, he realizes he wants to keep her safe…forever.

**Look for**

## An Unexpected Suitor

**by**

# ANNA SCHMIDT

*Available October wherever books are sold.*

Steeple
Hill®

LIH-82821

# *Love Inspired*
# SUSPENSE

## TITLES AVAILABLE NEXT MONTH

### Available October 13, 2009

**HEARTS IN THE CROSSHAIRS by Susan Page Davis**

She came to be inaugurated—and left dodging bullets.
Dave Hutchins of Maine's Executive Protection Unit doesn't
know who wants to kill governor Jillian Goff. Still, he won't
let her get hurt on his watch, not even when he finds his
own heart getting caught in the crosshairs.

**GUARDED SECRETS by Leann Harris**

"If I die, it won't be an accident." Lilly Burkstrom can't
forget her ex-husband's words...especially after his
"accidental" death. As her fear builds, the only person this
single mother can trust is Detective Jonathan Littledeer.
Can he keep Lilly safe?

**TRIAL BY FIRE by Cara Putman**

Her mother's house was first. Then her brother's. County
prosecutor Tricia Jamison is sure she's next on the arsonist's
list. But who is after her family? And why does every fire
throw her in the path of Noah Brust, the firefighter who
can't forgive or forget their shared past?

**DÉJÀ VU by Jenness Walker**

Cole Leighton can barely believe it when a woman on his
bus is abducted—in an *exact* reflection of a scene from the
bestseller he's reading. Someone's bringing the book to life...
and Kenzie Jacobs is trapped in the grisly story. Now the
killer is writing his own ending, and none of the twists and
turns lead to happily ever after.

LISCNMBPA0909